Training Session, Deadly Obsession

AC Knight

Published by AC Knight, 2022.

This is a work of fiction. Similarities to real people, places, or events are entirely coincidental.

TRAINING SESSION, DEADLY OBSESSION

First edition. October 27, 2022.

ISBN: 979-8215508312

Written by AC Knight.

To my husband, thank you for believing in this talent I'm trying to perfect. You are and have always been my biggest support system. For that, I am forever grateful. I love you.

To Martin, I love and miss you dearly.

To All, thank you for the support.

Chapter 1

"You know...we could have been so fuckin perfect together...you just had to FUCK it all up!" Katt said holding a combat knife to my neck as I sat helpless in the chair, she'd managed to tie me to. My head was still pounding from whatever she used to knock me out with. I felt stinging on my heels from what I'm assuming was her dragging me to this point. I struggled looking around trying to figure out my surroundings but was interrupted by Katt snatching my face. She forced me to look her in the eyes.

"You've been trying to sabotage everything between us for the last couple of months Al. I just don't understand... Please help me to understand because I LOVE YOU!" she said with that deranged look in her eyes I'd seen twice before.

"Katt...before you do anything crazy just calm down...tell me...where we are..." I pleaded trying to sooth her madness while inconspicuously trying to loosen the tape she wrapped around my wrist.

"Oh, you don't recognize where we are...this is where we first made love...the first moment I tasted the sweet nectar of your soul..." she said stepping from in front of me revealing the home I'd seen several times before during our affair. It was usually immaculate but now a disaster, representing the state of mind my once well put together lover.

"Listen, I know you're upset, but we can talk about this...where is he?" I asked still struggling to break the tape.

"That's the thing Al, I'm done talking...don't worry about him...I feel like if I can't have you...no one can..." she said as her voice trembled while waving the knife she once held to my neck. Those were the last word I heard before she knocked me out again.

Like the cliché line first line of a BET movie, I bet you're wondering how I ended up here? It's simple, I thought I could have my cake and eat it too, but this cake led to a deadly case of diabetes, type two to be exact, and what I'm sure would be the death of me. Before I die though, I'll walk you through the events that landed me here.

Chapter 2

My name is Allison Ferg, "Al" for short. At the age of 28, I found my calling in life. Before that, I went through several career changes. At one point, I wanted to be a cop. That was when I was a kid and cops weren't viewed as the enemy in my eyes. I went to a university to study criminal justice briefly before my financial situation took a shit. Sadly, I had to leave after an extremely successful semester. Back at home in Chicago while living with my dad, I had trouble finding a steady job. I had several jobs ranging from customer service to human resources. It was like nothing kept me interested long enough to stay. I was bored and broke so I decided to join the military.

After a year of waiting, I was accepted into the United States Navy and was off to bootcamp. I had the goal of keeping a steady job, using the benefits they offered, and travel to experience the world.

After four years of serving on board a ship based in Norfolk, Virginia, I decided it was time to call it quits. I received an honorable discharge and made Virginia my home. Once I was settled, I began using my education benefits known as the GI BILL. It was free money for school for up to three years. I decided to study aviation maintenance because it would be a simple transition from my experience while I served. I spent a year and a half learning, then landed a job working on aircrafts right after I graduated. I quickly found out I hate the work. Like being in the service, it was too demanding. I'm not sure why I expected different, silly me.

After a year of grinding it out at a local airport, I quit. It was back to the drawing board for me.

I almost forgot to mention, the entire time, Jeffrey, my husband was right by my side. We met in high school but remained friends until after I dropped out of college. He was the only person I could count to support me emotionally and somewhat financially. We dated for two years when he popped the question before I left for bootcamp. We got married while I was on leave (vacation for service members) and ever since, we've been inseparable. When I was on a boat halfway across the world, he was the only person I thought of and wanted to talk to. He was pretty much my first real love. He was my first in everything. I had never *been* with anyone else besides him. At the time I was sure I wanted no one else but him.

In my years of knowing Jeffrey, he was always sure of himself. He knew what he wanted to do with his life and made things happen for himself. After years of working three jobs and grinding through college, he earned his bachelor's degree in cyber security. Shortly after, he began making good money. He supported us both when I quit my job. He was always patient, trying his best to help me figure out career goals. One day, he caught me in our home gym going hard with my work out routine. I was very much in "the zone", I didn't notice he was watching me.

"You know, you work out like crazy, maybe you should become a personal trainer." He casually suggested.

"Personal trainer? Like helping of shape people and shit?" I said in the middle of a squat.

"Yes, I think that's more of your thing babe, it's something I've noticed you would be good at." he smiled. I took that suggestion and ran with it.

After all, I'd been working out since I was 16 years old and excelled in every physical activity I tried. I was told by several coaches and family members that I was a natural gifted athlete. I was one of the top recruits in my bootcamp division when it came to any physical readiness assessment. This did great things for my ego but it never occurred to me I could make money from helping people get fit. Jeffrey's words of encouragement were much needed.

Once again, I decided to use my G.I Bill to take some personal training courses offered at the local community college in my neighborhood. I completed the courses in six months without skipping a beat. I loved learning about nutrition, the psychology behind physical activity and the biology of the human body. As informative as these classes were, they didn't automatically make me a personal trainer. They were to prepare me for the exam to become certified. When I felt I was prepared, I took the ACE personal training certification exam. I passed on the first try. It took me about seven months to find a job at a big-time gym around a bunch of white folks in the Virginia Beach area.

After a year of establishing myself, I began a parttime business as a freelance trainer. I mainly worked with people from their homes. It was working out so well, I decided to expand back home in Chicago. I traveled back and forth while working around my day jobs and Va clients. It was really good money but most importantly I was finally enjoying what I was doing for a living.

Chapter 3

I've always thought I was built like a light skinned Serena Williams in a compact body, being that I was only five foot two inches. My face was round but chiseled once you reached my jaw line. My cheek bones were medium high with tiny freckles that complimented them. My locks were down the center of my back. I grew my locks after I was discharged from the service. It was a long, sometimes tedious, journey but it was worth it. They became a part of my fitness image. I enjoy taking pictures along with making videos of them swinging while demonstrating my workout routines for my social media followers. I never shied away from the fact that I was attractive but I kept a humble quiet confidence about me.

As you can imagine, my looks were sometimes distracting for my male clients. It didn't help that I never wore my wedding ring while at work. It was a hazard for me. I was always afraid I'd lost it going to the bathroom or something. However, respecting my husband, I always ignored their advances always keeping it professional. If I took on male clients during home visits, I'd make sure to bring my taser and keep an eye out for *extremely* inappropriate behavior. I rarely had any issues though.

During my primary job at the gym, I ran into a variety of clients; those who were generally concerned about their health, those trying to get fit because of a bet, and those who were seasonal gym rats. Seasonal gym rats, you know, the ones who always make it their new year's resolution to get in the gym but only go for a week or two before making up every excuse as to why they don't come back. They typically annoy me, but once the paycheck clears, I always think *"Well, I guess I'll see them same time next year."*

Everyone I worked with was cool, but I had one coworker whom I became best friends with. Her name was Nya, and like me, she was former navy who also decided to settle in Virginia. She's originally from Queens, New York and proudly boasted about how it's the greatest city in the world. She was a skinny dark-skinned girl with a face resembling a young Naomi Campbell while rocking a naturally short afro. She was a group instructor who taught a dance workout routine like Zumba but coined it "Nya's Rumba". People, especially older white women, loved it. Her energy was what attracted me to her as a friend. She was tough, outspoken, and assertive but was a sweetheart once you got to know her. She was also a "ride or die" friend. She would always suggest that I be more vocal and hardcore with my clients, but I had a quiet confidence as a trainer as well as in life. I believe my clients appreciated that.

I never yelled at them or got intense to motivate them. In a soft-spoken voice like Janet Jacksons singing voice, I'd say, *"Do you want this or not? Do you want to better your health or not? Because I'm getting exhausted from how you are wasting my time."* You can imagine how well that went over with some clients but most of them responded to this quiet harsh tactic by pushing themselves as hard as they could. That aspect of the job made it easier for me to love what I was doing for a living. It was very rewarding to see people push themselves towards a healthier life. Lord knows it takes strength and commitment to avoid falling into the statistics of adult obesity in the United States.

Everyday I'd usually get home before Jeffrey. I loved our house from the very moment we viewed it. We purchased it right after I was hired at the gym using my VA loan. It was a unique shade of green on the outside, two stories, four bedrooms, two baths, with a huge backyard. I always viewed it as our starter home because we eventually wanted at least two kids running around.

When I walked through the front door, I'd take some time to unwind from the day, dropping my gym bag and kicking my shoes off. I'd check my phone for text and voicemail messages left from potential clients because I seldomly checked my phone at the gym. (I found it distracting at the gym.)

I'd usually have two to four people requesting in-home sessions between VA and Chicago. I'd work around my regular work schedule to accommodate my clients for my business. I read a text from a woman named Katt Murphey. It seemed to be flirtatious in nature.

"Hello, Al, is it ok if I call you Al even though we haven't officially met lol Well, I'm contacting to schedule an appointment for Sunday at two thirty pm, please give me a text back at your earliest convenience...I've seen your arms on your Instagram... I'm looking forward to that work...out...thank you in advance, love."

I looked at my arms, flattered for some strange reason. I've received compliments many times from men but never from a woman...it was interesting.

After reading her message, I wrote all request dates and times down in my calendar and contacted everyone back. All perspective clients answered me back except Katt Murphey. I gave her a call, leaving a voicemail.

"Hello Ms. Murphey, thanks for calling Allison's Personal Training Sessions, just letting you know I have you book for two thirty pm Sunday and will arrive 10 minutes in advance. By the way, thanks for the compliment on my arms and of course you're welcomed to call me Al, it's sort of a nickname for me. Thank you for choosing my services. I'll see you Sunday."

I sat my phone down, took a quick shower, and started dinner. Jeffrey always strolled in the door right before I was finished cooking. He was such a beautiful man. He always impressed me with his simplicity. He always kept a nice button up top, alternating colors, with black slacks and black dress shoes. He enjoyed a bit of designer, but his closet wasn't full of name brands. He missed six feet coming in at five foot eleven inches. His caramel complexion complemented his neatly trimmed beard and short fade, kind of like Ghost AKA Omari Hardwick from the show Power. His beautiful brown eyes always seemed lighter when lights hit them. His body was muscular with a tiny case of "beer gut" but nonetheless he was extremely athletic. I loved the muscles on his back it was my favorite part of his body. Every time he walked through the door, I'd hug and kiss him, making sure I slowly ran my fingers down the well-defined structure of his back.

"Hey babe, how was your day?" he'd always beat me to the question in between kisses.

"It was fine, as always, living the fit life, ya know. How was yours?" I'd ask, then he'd smile and say, "Same old same old. Trying to keep the cyber world a safer place."

Then we'd briefly part ways while I finished up dinner as he began unwinding from his day. His pattern was getting undressed, showering then getting comfortable at the kitchen table patiently waiting for the food to be finished. After dinner, we'd talk more about our day while sipping on some red wine then we'd catch up on our favorite tv shows then finally retire to bed.

This was our routine. There were some days we'd have sex then there were days we didn't. We'd go through weird droughts, then we'd be all over each other like two jack rabbits after my work travel from Chicago. In time, I chalked it up to us being in a long-term relationship.

Jeffrey was my first and only He virtually taught me all the sex positions one person could teach another. He knew every inch of my body. The sex was amazing in the beginning, but us being together for so long, I became bored.

I looked up some things to spice up the bedroom like toys, kinks, and bondage. He was caught off guard by this. He told me being tied down "wasn't his thing" because he wouldn't feel in control. He said he also wouldn't feel right doing it to me. Kinks were out of the question because it was "mad weird". Apparently, we didn't need toys because he swore up and down, he was good enough alone to pleasure me. I even brought up the idea of having sex in public but he had a bad experience as a teen that almost resulted in arrest for indecent exposure.

"The bedroom is the only place your ass should be clapping! Babe, why would I want you to be anyone else other than you? This version of you I'd the only one that makes my dick hard! Look at it, it's rising as we speak. You being you is the absolute best, I'm not down with that extra stuff." he'd explain.

"How would you know if we never tried?" I'd challenge.

"I know because I find you perfect the way you are. I find our sex life perfect the way it is. I know for a fact I still do it for you. Orgasms don't lie" he'd say.

"If you say so." I'd say thinking about the most recently faked orgasm. Then the discussion would suddenly end.

After a while, I gave up on the idea of any excitement in the bedroom. Since we had no kids or pets to provide some form of entertainment, I forced myself to be content with our increasingly boring sex life. What else was I to expect from a man that was stuck in his ways sexually? That was something I probably should have pushed for more because then maybe, I wouldn't have ended up in such a fucked-up situation.

Chapter 4

Katt Murphey finally called back to confirm our appointment. When I talked to her, she was rambling, appearing to be preoccupied. It wasn't anything new for me, I was used to clients rushing me off the phone to tend to their busy lives. Oddly, I was looking forward to our session. I thought about the compliment she'd given my arms and how she called me by my nickname before ever meeting.

Sunday arrived, Katt Murphey was the only one on my calendar for that day. After I made breakfast, I began to pack my training bag. When I met clients at their home for the first time, I usually packed light even during trips to Chicago. The first session was always about documenting their overall fitness goals while measuring their current level of fitness. I packed light dumb bells, resistance bans, a ten-pound kettle bell, and a yoga mat just in case they didn't have one of their own. I didn't require my clients to have a "fitness space" in their house. I worked with whatever space they gave me which was wherever they were comfortable seeing sweat drop. I wore my signature green compression shorts underneath my "coochie cutter" jogging shorts for support and comfort. I also wore my grey compression shirt that complimented my arms and showed off the outline of my abdominal muscles. I pulled my locks back into a simple ponytail while checking myself out in our bedroom mirror.

The clock read one forty-five pm when I started to GPS where Katt Murphey lived. To my delight, she was only twenty minutes away from where we lived. Some of my clients lived forty minutes to an hour away in Virginia. Traffic could be brutal depending on the time of day, but this was Sunday, traffic was going to be nonexistent. When two o'clock rolled around, I let Jeffrey know I was leaving as he sat half naked on our living room couch in his favorite pair of blue boxer briefs. I gave him a quick kiss as he sat fixated on his video game mashing buttons before glancing up as I walked out the front door.

"Be safe." I heard him say as I closed the door hopping into my Chevrolet Impala.

The ride to Katt Murphey's house was smooth as I predicted. When I pulled into her driveway I noticed her car, a white 2018 BMW M3 CS. This meant she had *money*. Majority of my clients had good money which usually meant big tips, so this relationship was already starting off on a good foot. She had a ranch style home with a one car garage connected. I wondered what she kept in her garage to have such a nice ass car parked in the driveway exposed to the unpredictable weather in VA.

I glanced at the clock on my phone as it read two nineteen pm while making my way to her front door ringing the doorbell.

"One second!" she yelled rushing to open the door. I was greeted by her in coveralls covered in a mixture of acrylic paint colors dried and wet. She was undoubtably gorgeous. She was my age, standing about five foot three inches, with natural hair in the form of a tall curly afro with honey blonde dye at the tips. Her skin was a flawless mocha complexion, her eyes were a unique shade of blue making it hard to tell if they were real or not, and her body was slim with a slight plump in her breast and butt.

She reminded me of a young Nia long. I was considerably taken back by her beauty, my face flushed red with blush. She noticed.

"Oh shit, Al, I mean Mrs. Allison", she smiled rubbing the fresh paint from her right hand frantically onto her coveralls, "I swear, I completely forgot you were coming! Shit, I forgot to remind myself! Damn you look better in person, I followed you on your Instagram if you hadn't noticed. Please, please come in, don't mind the paint, I got really focused on a project I've been working on." She said gesturing with her now semi dry hand to come in.

"Are you sure because we can reschedule if you're really busy." I suggested still blushing. She would have no part of that idea, after all she did make it a point to confirm.

"No, no really come in! I need to put work aside to get my health in order, you know? That's why I called you in first place, please come in. You can make yourself comfortable in my living room, I just need to wash my hands and change into my work out clothes. Oh my god, I'm so excited you're here, I'm ready to sweat!" she said before turning to walk down into what I assumed was her master bedroom, being that I spotted two other doors in the narrow hallway.

As she suggested, I made myself comfortable on her brown plush couch. I began to observe her entire living space. It was extremely neat with variety of art hanging on the walls. She had a rug that was multicolored under a clear glass coffee table which I sat my bag on, then realized it was rude and immediately put it on the floor. I glanced behind me noticing she had an island counter in her kitchen. It had black marble tiling which was something I'd never seen before in a house. *"She must have remodeled"* I thought to myself.

She had these interesting life-like paintings of Maya Angelou and Malcom X. I wondered if they were of her own making or if she was a collector as I admired them. Ten minutes went by before she came into the living room with a red sports bra, red compression shorts (that were like mine) to match and random green puma sneakers. As she stood, I was still embarrassed about my blushing because I'd never had a client as beautiful as her.

"Wow, looks like you came prepared with that gear." I tried joking to mask my obvious attraction to her.

"Yea, it's something I've had stored in my dresser for a while", she shrugged. I took another look at her shoes and raised an eyebrow.

"What's the story with the shoes?" I asked trying not to sound judgmental, they seemed random to me.

She laughed, "I just like green, I know it doesn't match but never mind that! Let's get to it! Come on, make me sweat. Don't let my skinny frame fool you, I am out of shape! Painting is my thing but it doesn't keep me fit." She tilted her head placing both her hands on her hips.

"Hold on a second" I interrupted her, "We must get a few things on paper first."

"Ok, my bad, I'll bring it back, I really am sorry for the wait, you know how it is when you get really intense with your work, you forget everything that's going on around you." She explained. I nodded as I pulled out my note pad and pen.

"Yea, I get it...I get a little lost in my workouts."

"I can tell." She said smirking while seductively eyeballing my arms. I changed the topic before she could see the red in my face.

Clearing my throat, "So, we must go over some of your fitness goals first, then measure your level of fitness. Before we get to that, why don't you tell me a little bit about yourself? How did you decided that I was the one you would trust with your physical health?" I said in my professional voice.

"Well, I'm originally from Chicago, the Southside to be exact...I have a bachelor's degree in Art from Columbia College. As you can see, I'm a painter but I know how to use a camera as well. The portraits hanging are some of my original pieces." she said pointing to Maya Angelou, "I recently had a very successful show case in Chicago that got me paid, paid!" she said laughing.

"That's incredible, I'm from Chicago too, I travel back and forth for work there. This is crazy. How'd you end up in Virginia if you don't mind me asking?"

"Well, I had a boyfriend that was in the navy, but he..." she said with a sudden far out look in her eyes, "he um...cheated on me...it was a little hard to get over, I don't really like talking about it...but anyway here I am. I brought a home in Virginia because I liked it here, I find it peaceful. I decided I'd do some of my work here then travel to Chicago since I have the funds, you know." She explained

"That's cool, I can agree with the peace here. I guess it's the slow country lifestyle I love as well. I'm sorry about what happened between you and your ex. At least your art is dope."

"Yea, it is what it is...but here I am thriving, trying to get my body right!" she perked up, "I happened to be scrolling on Instagram and saw one your advertisements and decided to check you out. Has anyone ever told you look like a light skinned Serena Williams?", she smiled.

I laughed flattered at the irony she'd describe me like that, "Well, I thought you looked great. You seemed like a good match for me, the rest will be history because here you are, and I'm ready to get it in!" she said with excitement.

"Well, that's great, just know I'm here for every step of your journey, so let's get to work."

I asked her a few more questions about her fitness goals then proceeded with my personal physical fitness test in her spacious living room. She was nowhere near as out of shape as she said she was which made me think she was holding back. The 2-hour session was over before I knew it, and she seemed satisfied.

"Well, that was pretty good. You are great at what you do" she said sipping on a water she grabbed from her refrigerator. "Do you want a water?" she asked.

"Uh yea, I'll take one. This was good, one of the best I've had with a client at home. Are you sure you need me?" I joked.

She took another sip of water as sweat dripped down her neck "Oh yea, I'm sure..." she winked her right eye at me. There I was about to blush again.

"We'll this will cost you 350$, I take debit or cash." I said taking a sip of water. Katt walked a short distance to grab her bag from the kitchen table.

"Yes, of course, I have the cash right here." She said stepping towards me pulling out a wad of 100$ bills wrapped in a rubber band from her purse.

"Aw wow, I'm so sorry, I don't think I have change, I can swipe a card though." I said embarrassed remembering I left my change pouch at home.

"It's fine, take it, this a tip included transaction." She said smiling "Besides, you should remember your change the next session, right? I don't like to use cards." she said placing the money in my hand. I nodded my head yes, thanked her for her business, then headed for the front door. However, curiosity stopped me.

"You have a nice ass car, why isn't it in your garage? You know we're in Virginia, the weather is crazy here." I laughed, she giggled.

"As you can see, this house is a "little big house" so I keep the rest of my art in the garage...you wanna check it out before you leave, or do you have another client to get to?" She asked gesturing to her garage door.

"No, you were my only client for the day, so why not, I love what I've seen so far." I said following her through the garage door. It was stacked with paintings upon paintings. Some of historical figures, some of regular people, and some were covered up. There were also nature photos which were breath taking.

"Those pictures are from when I went to India, the landscape there is amazing and the people, not so bad."

"These are amazing, they must be for your next show." I said admiring her work.

"Yea, some of them…" she said admiring her work while admiring me. Our eyes met which made me nervous.

"I should get going, my husband will probably be wondering about me." I said breaking our gaze.

"Husband? Not to be rude, but where's the ring? I don't see any evidence of him on your social media either." she asked raising her eyebrows gently grabbing my right hand messaging my ring finger.

"I don't wear it while I'm working or working out. Don't want to damage it, you know. I just keep things private with us everything isn't for the internet's consumption." I said shrugging my shoulders gently pulling away from her hand.

"Uh huh" she said smirking "that's a damn good reason, your husband must be a very secure man to let you walk around like that."

"Yea, he's solid…" I said locking eyes with her again, "Well, I guess I'll see you next weekend, same time?" I said signaling it was time for me to go.

"Yes, two thirty pm, I promise next time I won't be covered in paint" she laughed as she pushed the button to open her garage door. I thanked her once again while rushing to my car. I waved goodbye and drove home doing a little over the speed limit.

I'd never been around a client that made me so excitingly nervous, let alone a woman. There was something strange about her energy, I enjoyed it. I thought to myself, maybe it was her art or maybe it was her eyes, then again could have been her lips. Whatever it was, she had me hot all the way until I pulled into my driveway.

"Hey, babe" Jeffrey greeted me as I walked through the door "How was work?"

"It was great, my new client is pretty cool." I said sitting my bag on the living room floor.

"That's good babe, why don't you get on in the shower and come down here and watch a movie with me." he said patting his hand on the side of our grey couch.

"Yea ok, just give me a minute." I said making my way up the stairs to our bedroom.

My shower took longer than usual. I found myself replaying Katts features in my head on a loop as I almost began to touch myself. Her lips, her smirk, and the sweat running down her neck. It was doing something to me.

"What's really going on?" I thought out loud as water ran down my face and chest, drips trickling off my nipples, as I watch the water spiral down the drain.

I usually told Jeffrey every detail of my training sessions, but for some reason I was reluctant to expand on this one. I didn't know if it was from my undeniable attraction that grew stronger by the minute or because I was afraid of how he would react to me sharing that a woman was flirting with me. I wasn't sure, but this was the first time I kept something from my husband. This was also the first time I ever got out of the shower dripping wet, lust in my eyes, rushing to mount my husband because of how turned on I was. What he didn't know certainly didn't hurt him.

Chapter 5

Business went as usual for the next few months. I had my regular clients during the week at the gym and my side clients traveling between VA and Chicago. Katt became one of my most consistent clients in VA. I began to look forward to our sessions as we became closer. I found myself bringing her up at random times with Jeffrey, he could tell I was excited about this new client. I knew her life story and she knew mine.

Art was her calling which saved her from depression rooted in childhood trauma. The results were her no longer being close to her family, particularly her mother. She came from money but achieved her dreams of success as a painter in a short period of time. The loneliness she felt disappeared with the more money she made. She seemed happy every time I saw her until one day, she threw me for a loop.

When I pulled into her driveway around the usual time, I noticed her front door cracked opened. I grabbed my taser from my training bag and cautiously entered her home.

"Hey, Katt! You alright? The door was open...Katt!?" I shouted looking around. I walked into her bedroom only to find her on her bed passed out with a bottle of pills sprawled out on her nightstand. I rushed over to her trying to shake awake. I slapped her face frantically shouting her name until she regained consciousness.

"Katt? Katt? What the hell did you take?!" I questioned practically panicking.

"Hhmm...wha...what are you talking about its fine..." she groaned pushing me away as she began to come back to life, "They're sleeping pills Al...hmmm I was having trouble sleeping this week..." she groaned.

"Why was your front door open?!" I asked catching my breath while simultaneously flopping on the edge of her bed.

"Oh, I guess I forgot to close it when the pizza man came...damn, I wasn't supposed to tell you that...I'm not trying to do twenty burpees today." She yarned while rubbing her eyes, seemingly more concerned about the punishment over empty carbs.

"You just scared the shit out of me." I confessed with a tremble in my voice.

"Oh shit, my bad Al, damn you came up in here tryna save a bitch and shit." She joked.

"Yea, I was one minute away from using my CPR certification." I laughed nervously.

"Oh, really" she said yarning still laying comfortably on her back, "that's that mouth-to-mouth stuff huh?" she smiled looking up at me. There she was again flirting with me, forcing me to acknowledge with a smirk.

"Yea, mouth to mouth BREATHING, with chest compressions." I said trying to keep things professional.

"Sounds kinky." She joked forcing me to laugh. I stood up reaching for the taser I dropped on the floor from my initial shock.

"Oh wow, you REALLY were about to fuck some shit up." She said finally sitting up to get a better look at me in my "super save a hoe" stance.

"Can't ever be too prepared. I remember us discussing you dealing with depression. I also think you forgot we're from Chicago, ain't nothing good about opened doors. You know we lock our shit up. I didn't know what I was walking into, people on VA forget to lock everything up, it's weird to me." I said fascinated by her blue eyes. She was wearing nothing but a blue laced bra with panties to match. I found myself looking for an excuse to escape her bedroom

"Look, I'm going to go. I don't think you need to work out today, sleeping pills slow you down, wouldn't be a good idea, you know?" I explained.

"Al wait come here..." she said patting her pillow signaling for me to sit down. I acknowledged her request choosing to stand with my arms crossed next to her bed.

"I know I told you I suffered from depression and shit, but I really am okay now. I seriously have trouble sleeping sometimes. I saw a doctor about it, here you can check the pills for the prescription." She pleaded while shaking the bottle for me to check.

"Listen, I believe you, but I keep telling you these pills aren't going to solve your sleeping issues. I have more natural ways that could help you."

"Yea, I bet you do...but I like quick solutions for certain things, sleep is one of them." She said still yarning, "Since, you say we can't work out, might as well chill then. Allison, you basically almost saved my life. I wasn't in danger though but I really appreciate your concern."

"Yea, well these are business hours, not "hang out and chill" hours." I said sternly while trying to ignore her body in her lingerie.

"Listen, I'll still pay you for your time, but any time after that is off the clock, ok? So, get your ass in the living room and relax while I get myself together. We can have some on the clock off the clock girl time. How does that sound?" she coaxed me to agree.

"I guess." I agreed reluctantly uncrossing my arms, exiting her bedroom to make myself comfortable.

I made a quick sprint to my car to return my taser. When I returned, I plopped on her plush brown couch. I noticed some new paintings hanging.

"Is this some of your new stuff?!" I yelled loud enough for her to hear from her bedroom.

"Yea, what do you think about them?!" she responded from the shower.

I stood up to get a better look at a painting with a woman posing half nude with a green silk robe. There were poses of her completely nude in various positions on four other canvases. My eyes weren't deceiving me, the woman shared a strong resemblance to me. I was creeped out yet flattered. I must admit I was more flattered than anything. I could only assume that I was the inspiration behind these new pieces.

"I like them...they are pretty...dope." I yelled as she made her way into the living room. She was still damp with her body wrapped in a bathing towel.

"Yea, they are dope. You know were my muse." She confessed winking at me on her way to the kitchen.

As I said, we'd been getting to know each other for some time now. She briefly spoke on her ex-boyfriend and the topic of sexuality obviously came up. The flirting was very consistent on her part, so it prompted me to probe a little bit more into her background.

"So... was your last break up really that bad? What happened? You never touched on it...Are you like...attracted to women too?" I rambled off.

Katt giggled as she opened her refrigerator, grabbing some water and a bottle of wine. I was positive she was aware of wine and sleep pills not mixing well.

"Allison, I'm bisexual. I feel like I made that obvious. You know damn well I've been flirting with you this entire time. My guess was that either you like it or you're too nice to tell me to stop...My ex was a cheating asshole. He hurt me down to my core. That's the end of that story." she replied searching for her wine opener.

"Yea, I guess I was well aware...and I am too nice...I mean, I guess I didn't know how to take it...Usually, I don't pay it any mind..." I confessed, "Hey, um, you're not going to drink that are you? Please don't tell me you're mixing those pills with wine." I shifted my concern.

She smirked as she found the wine opener from the drawer she'd been searching for. She inserted the opener in the cork, popping it like a seasoned pro. She grabbed a glass from her dish drying rack and poured halfway to the rim.

"I know you're my personal trainer and we might be becoming good friends but you're not my mother, so I'm going to need for you to calm down." She checked me while taking another sip. She grabbed another glass pouring it half full again.

"I know that... I'm just saying it's a health concern for me. I wouldn't feel right if I didn't speak up about it." I urged.

She stepped over to me, still moist from the shower handing me the glass which I shamefully accepted.

"Look, this is my personal training time, ok, and you're most likely right when it comes to health stuff, but I'm the one paying you right now, you feel me." she said continuing to sip, "Just relax like I keep trying to tell you. Take a sip. I know some of you health professional still drink occasionally."

I couldn't argue with her, after the scare she gave me, I was due for a sip or two. I watched as she went back to her room to change, glass still in hand. She came back in a white tank top, no bra, and green booty shorts that fit her figure perfectly. She joined me on the couch, noticing I'd made myself at home. She smelled like a wonderful combination of lemons and shea butter. I glanced at her trying to avoid eye contact because she was once again forcing me to blush.

"You sure did have a lot of questions today. Does it freak you out that I used you as inspiration for my work? I think you're sexy and that coming from me as a friend." She said still sipping. I drank along with her, trying to focus on the rim of the glass.

"I see you're avoiding eye contact. Your high yellow ass is always blushing, so I know you're not just being nice. You're just being a weirdo about being attracted to another woman," she chuckled, "I know you're married and love your husband Al, you've been doing the strictly dickly thing all your life. That's ok."

I was embarrassed at how obvious my attraction to her was. She was reading me the entire time. She sensed my curiosity, yea, I was terrible at hiding it.

"Well, your paintings are interesting, I never envisioned being painted naked by a friend. You have an amazing imagination. And yes, I am very much strictly dickly." This was hilarious to her.

"I'm an artist! I've seen myself in PLENTY of pieces naked that were made by friends. Imagination is apart of the artistry. That's what makes us special. I was always flattered to be honest...Are you sure you just like the dick...I guess I'll have to believe you." She winked with a hint of sarcasm taking a few more big sips, "Just admit you like the attention, then I'll leave it alone."

I nodded and took another small sip as we giggled together.

We continued talking for almost six hours. I was now three glasses in feeling good. Katt was now noticeably tipsy. I suspected she still had some pills left over in her system. She slurred her words all the while becoming touchy. I didn't mind, I enjoyed spending this time with her. Realty set in when I got a text from Jeffrey. He was wondering where I was and if I was ok. I told him I was fine, off the clock, just hanging out. I left out the part about being with Katt. Always trusting my word, he told me to let him know when I was on my way home.

"That's the hubby, huh?" she asked as I texted.

"Yea...he worries. I should probably be getting out of here." I stood up. Katt gently took my hand looking up at me and said, "Five more minutes, please. I'm going to have to wait an entire week to see you again."

"Well yea, Sundays are the days you have me." I said still trying to maintain my false sense of professionalism.

"Does your husband know? Does he know you... might like me?" she suggested. I pulled away from her hand as I began to make my way towards the front door. I must have been moving in slow motion because I allowed her to stop me. I paused as she pressed her hand against my chest preventing my exit.

"Hold on, look I didn't mean it like that, I was just asking if he knew we were friends?" she explained going for my hands again. She looked me in the eyes and pulled me close.

"I mean...he knows you're one of my most reliable clients, I tell him a little about you, so I guess yes, why?" I asked breathlessly pulling away once again but the wine was taking over me.

"Hmm most reliable...client... just curious because I don't want to be a secret, ya know."

This moment was too much for me. I had to get out of there and home to my husband to unleash everything this moment was building up inside of me.

"Look Katt, I really must go...just make sure you take it easy on the sleeping pills and wine. And for god's sake, please don't mix them. I'll see you next Sunday." I said making another attempt to leave by pushing her out the way. She blocked me again, pulling me towards her, guiding my lips to hers. I could still taste the wine on her soft plump lips as she guided her tongue onto mine. She took me over, pushing me against her front door. She began to run her hands slowly up and down my body, caressing my breast, all the while kissing me passionately. Those three glasses allowed this to happen, I enjoyed every forbidden second of it. She knew I was loose and took full advantage of it. I had to stop her once her hand started to glide towards my vagina.

"Yo...um, Katt, listen, I really have to go..." I plead in a trance of passion.

"Hmm, do you really? I bet if I tasted your pussy right now, you'd be saying something different." She whispered biting her lip then mine. I was on fire and ready to take a plunge into this abyss of ecstasy, but the discipline I had prevailed. I pushed her away connecting with her beautiful eyes to show her enough was enough. She backed off still biting her bottom lip with her hand propped above her right breast.

"Oh yea, the husband...", she sighed, "Ok...I guess, I'll see you next Sunday."

I nodded as I bolted out the front door. "That was too much." I said to myself in disbelief as I jumped in my car. I placed my hands inside my pants to feel myself. I was sure for the first time in my life I squirted. Taking deep breathes, I tried to calm myself down before I was on the road. I contemplated "What if I stayed?". That wasn't an option because my husband was at home waiting for me. This happened. I let her seduce me and...I liked it. I liked it a lot.

When I finally got home, Jeffrey was in the shower. I ambushed him while I was still fully clothed, giving him the best head of his life while water ran down both our bodies. We fucked for almost two hours that day. Afterwards, I felt so guilty, I decided to burry my shame deep within. It was too much, but I liked it...I really liked it.

Chapter 6

I decided to skip my next two appointments with Katt, opting to travel to Chicago instead. She called a couple of times, I ignored them all. Jeffrey didn't notice how distracted I was as we spent our normal time together. He eventually noticed I stopped bringing up Katt Murphy as often. I told him she canceled a few appointments which is what clients do from time to time. Nya, on the other hand, was on to my ass. She could sense my energy was off but couldn't put a finger on it. Being Nya, she was going to pry until I gave her answers.

"Girl, for the twentieth time, what the hell has been your problem? Your clients are up in here reminding you of your damn workout routines. That's not like you, so what's the tea? Jeffrey been acting up or something?" she pressed while we were lounging at our desk.

"Nya, please. I told you I'm fine, I've been trying to come up with some new routines for my some of my clients, I'm getting them confused mixed up. I just need to get things organized in my head." I explained but she wasn't hearing it.

"In all the time I've known you, you've never had things "mixed up" let alone routines, YA LYIN!" she exclaimed calling me out on my bullshit.

"Shhhh, the hell is wrong with you?" I tried silencing her while looking around to see if any was eavesdropping on our conversation.

"Are you serious right now? Half these people in here have headphones on! Talkin bout shh!" she said glaring at me like I was stupid. I buried my face in my hands exhausted from her prying.

"Ok then, I have to tell you something...PLEASE don't judge..." I begged.

"Girl when have you ever known me to do that?"

I sighed whispering as she drew herself closer, "A couple of weeks ago...a client of mine came on to me...hard." I confessed. Nya's right eyebrow jumped to the top of her forehead causing her ears to perk up along with them.

"How are hard we talkin?" she asked, leaning in closer. I let out another sigh, "She...kissed me."

"SHE?!" she said blurted. I smacked my lips, "You JUST said you weren't going to judge! Why you still being so damn loud!?" I said raising my voice still scanning the room for any nosy parties.

"I'm sorry this is catching me off guard, you know I'm always open to new things but you...you like girls now?" she finally tried her hand at whispering.

"How long have you known me? How long have I been married Nya? What kind of question is that?" I countered unsure of how to answer. After all, it was a very new experience for me. At the time I didn't know it wouldn't be the last.

"A long time...but you know...things change, people change...you could just be a tad bit curious at this point int your life." she said leaning back in her chair shrugging her shoulders.

"Listen, it was nothing, it meant nothing." I lied.

"Uh huh, if that's the case, why have you been so off lately? Another thing I want to know is, does Jeffrey know?" she asked. I didn't know which question to answer first so I avoided answering either by turning to my computer and acting like I was checking my email.

"Oh, so it's like that Allison?" she laughed. I rolled my eyes, turning back around to confess, "Look, the whole thing was confusing for me. Ever since I took her own as a client, she's had my full attention, nose wide open Nya, and this shit is strange for me. I'm sitting here like "what the fuck is going on with me?" You know damn well Jeffrey is my everything, my only thing, but this woman has been fucking with my head. I've never been attracted to women but it's something about her that's draws me in and its scary. That's why I haven't seen her in weeks. I'm freaked out."

"I get it, I mean, it's interesting. Women are sexy, hell, you're a woman, you know! Wait, so you haven't seen her in weeks. That's unprofessional as hell, Al." She said smacking her lips.

"At this point, I don't think she cares about what's professional and what not professional Nya." I rolled my eyes.

"Hmm, yea you right, well that's a pickle girl. I would think you told Jeffrey everything...Honestly, I'm not sure why I had to twist your arm to get this information, she must be... special."

"She's an artist. She used me as inspiration for some of her work" I shrugged my shoulders thinking about her paintings.

"Ohhhh, well girl even male artists have some type of aura about them that's makes them irresistible to the trained eye. She's just from a different world and you, my friend, are just not use to that type of energy or never knew that you were attracted to that type of energy... What's her name? Now I must investigate, you know I'm about to go back to school for criminal justice and my new man, Todd, is a police officer in training, we must see who we are working with."

"You're saying that like I'm trying to get into a relationship her, I still view her as a client and friend... Most importantly, I'm married Nya, and married to the man whose children I want to have!" I passionately explained.

"Yea...but last time I checked you were bored in the bedroom... Did you or did you not tell me that? This woman could just be a project, ya know." She tilted her head.

I honestly couldn't believe what was coming out of her mouth.

"So, your saying, I should keep her as a client?" I asked for clarification.

"Yes of course, just set boundaries or not... whatever works for you that day..." she sarcastically joked.

"I can't believe you're basically telling me to cheat on my husband, this is insane." I said up in arms.

"No, I didn't, and you most definitely did NOT hear those word come out of my mouth. What's her name? I'm going to look her up on social media, if I find something off, you know I'll tell you." she said turning to her computer to pull up Instagram.

"Her name is Katt Murphey...she should be following me." I whispered pulling my chair closer to hers in view of her computer screen.

"Aw yeaaa, her she is...well damn, she's gorgeous! No wonder, you're all messed up. All confused and shit! I'd give her some go too...", she laughed scrolling through her page, "Her art is dope too.... I see she's from Chicago, hmmm."

"Yea, she's from the southside too."

"Fascinating."

"So, we can really relate...you know."

"I bet yall bond over gunshots and deep dish pizza...ha ha." She teased but the joke didn't land for me.

"Ok, chill..." I scooted away from her as she continued to study her page.

"Ha ha! CHIRAQ!! Come on now, you know I'm just kidding. She is very beautiful though and very talented...crazy...I'm not encouraging thot-ish behavior because I know you're *happily* married. I'm just going to suggest you be careful and try to continue a client relationship and possibly a friendship because she has MONEY. You shouldn't miss out on that. Just tell your hormones to chill and save it for the hubby, you feel me?" she said providing a solution.

"That's another thing so far, every time I've left her, I go home and fuck the shit out of Jeffrey. I want to do different things with him, but he's just not into it." I sadly confessed.

"Well, I'm not sure what else to tell you girl. You're your own woman and you know what's right, what's wrong, and what's worth it. Just know I would never judge, and I can keep a secret." she said turning to me, closing out Katt's page. I shared a faint look of doom, but Nya placed her hand on my shoulder, "Everything will be fine. Just keep it professional and friendly but not "*too too*" friendly. By the way, I need to meet her, got to get a feel for the girl, you know, if you decide she's worth it."

"I guess..." I said returning to my computer.

I thought about what Nya said. I did need to keep it professional. Being real with myself, I knew it wasn't very professional to ghost her. She did have money that could be in my pockets. However, I really enjoyed her company as a friend. It wouldn't have hurt to keep that going, *so I thought*.

I was still unsure about telling Jeffrey everything about Katt Murphey. I rationalized it in my head, "*It was nothing but a tipsy kiss, he doesn't need to know that, why tell him?*". He'd probably laugh if I did tell him or, by the grace of God, finally want to do something interesting in the bedroom, a threesome maybe. *Or* he'd be furious, questioning our entire life together. I gave it a lot of though and ultimately decided against telling him anything. It was something I'd keep between myself...Nya...Katt...and God...Jeffery was forever forbidden from knowing.

Later that week, I decided to give Katt a call. To my surprise, she was happy to hear from me, sounding busy as usual. I imagined her working on some new painting. She asked me to visit, not as her trainer but as a friend that Saturday. I was hesitant, but I thought "*why not?*". I had to apologize for my behavior. I had the dilemma of trying to escape my husband without stirring up suspicion.

When I got home, I decided to go with some half-truths to see my secret lover/friend. I told him while training, we'd become friends and she'd canceled on me before because her work schedule picked up. I told him that she'd told me that everything was now slowing down for her so she'd have to time to see me again.

"Ok babe, it's good to see you're making new friends. Nya is starting to annoy me." he joked kissing my forehead as we laid in bed.

"Yea... just letting you know, I won't know what time I'll be getting back in, it's going to be a girl's night." I said as he flicked off the lamp on the nightstand.

"That's cool, I'll be out with some of the guys. It's fine babe, besides I think we spend too much time together anyway", he laughed climbing back in bed, "it's healthy to hang out with other people so we don't get tired of each other."

"You're absolutely right." I said watching him pull the covered over his shoulders as he began to close his eyes.

"I love you."

"Love you too." I whispered back, then proceeded to toss and turn the entire night barely sleeping.

Chapter 7

Saturday evening arrived; Jeffrey was already at one of his homeboy's homes as he said he would. I was left alone to get ready for my night with Katt. I had a hard time deciding what to wear because subconsciously I wanted to impress her. She hadn't seen me in anything other than my gym clothes. Not to mention, I rarely post myself cleaned up on social media. I didn't know whether to keep it casual or get dolled up.

I convinced myself to keep it casual. My casual was a black and white fitted dress with black semi high heels I purchased forever ago that were collecting dust. I twisted my locks into a tight bun that sat on top of my head. I glanced in the mirror approving the look while checking my shape. I made sure to slap on my wedding ring as a final touch before I hopped in my car, pulling up to Katts house in no time. I rang the doorbell, nervously waiting, wiping my hands on my butt to keep them from becoming too sweaty.

She opened the door in a red skin-tight dress with silver hoop earrings, making you pay more attention to her flawless make up, while her curly afro still mesmerized you. She wore red bottoms towering over me, greeting me with a hug and kiss.

"Well look at you, aren't you just so damn cute! Come in, you know where to go. I have a bottle of red open if you want some." She winked as I made my way to the living room. I watched as she glided to the kitchen.

"No, trust me, I'm good." I said sliding down on her couch.

"Oh yea...Listen, I'm sorry about what happened last time. It really was the side effects of those sleeping pills. I didn't mean to cross a line. I know you're trying to keep things professional...when you're working of course." She apologized, watching me from her kitchen counter. She then poured two glasses of wine.

"You didn't have to ghost me like that though", she said as she made her way over to me. Her figure was in my view as she balanced the two glasses in each hand, "Look, I gained about twenty pounds back." She proclaimed sarcastically while modeling for me. She was teasing me, anyone with eyes could see she hadn't gained a thought of a pound.

"You look fine to me..." I complemented, "I'm also sorry. I didn't mean to ghost you like that. I was..." she interrupted before I could finish my thought by handing me the glass of red I'd previously declined.

"Its okay Al, we were both tripping. It's water under the bridge now, forgotten, never thought of again, ok?" she assured me while taking a sip.

"I'll just take some water." I said sitting the glass on the dining room table

"Look at you, you must be a "*fool me once*" type of person." She said returning the glass to her kitchen. She returned with a bottle of water.

"So, I know I said we were going to chill at my place, but I double booked." She confessed

"How so?" I said taking a sip of water.

"Well, a friend of mine had some luck with a small venue, he begged me to show off some of my work. It's at this place called Oasis in downtown Virginia Beach, have you heard of it?" she asked.

"Yes, I think I drove by it a couple of times when I have clients out that was... I never knew it was a venue for art shows."

"VA Beach has a lot of low-key art shit going on there, you just have to know people that *know* people. Anyway, I have a tiny name for myself here that's why my friend is hosting this venue for some VA fans. Hopefully some of my work sales, when I say hopefully, I know in fact they will. I want you to come with me, it starts soon that's why I'm so dressed up." She said taking a sip then crossing her legs, watching for my response.

"Sounds interesting...I guess I'm down...Is what I'm wearing ok, I don't think I'm dressed for an art show."

"Dope...not to make you uncomfortable, but you look amazing", she said admiring my look "let's get ready to leave in a few, it's about a forty-minute drive. I like to get there a little early to check out the crowd, you know, to see if people notice me. Who am I kidding, of course they'll notice me, I'm the shit." she giggled.

"You know damn well they will." I agreed. I'd never been to an art show in my life, even if it was local one. I was curious to see what she'd be showing. Hopefully they were the ones inspired by me... how amazing it would be for me to be hanging on someone's wall.

"Cool, I'll drive and just so you know, I wasn't drinking until you got here. You literally saw me take a sip so I'm good to go." she said standing up to search for her keys.

"Uh huh, well I guess we'll find out." I said standing up with my half drunken battle of water.

"Girl, I am a safe driver, come on let's go." She said finding her keys and grabbing her purse from the stool next to the kitchen table.

We shuffled out the front door, hopping into her BMW. The inside was custom with black and white leather seats. It had a new car smell that surprised me.

"Did you just buy this car or something?" I asked buckling myself in the passenger seat.

"Nah, it always smells fresh for some reason." She giggled buckling herself in and starting the ignition.

We pulled out the driveway as she fumbled with her phone trying to pull up the GPS to guide us to our destination.

"So, what kind of music do you listen to? I don't think I've ever asked you that, we barely listen to music when we work out. If you did put something on, it was some generic "stomp to the beat" mess." she said glancing at me then refocusing on the road.

"I'm not particular, I'll give anything a chance, but I do enjoy a lot of R&B; new and old school, Hip-hop; new and old, sad boy/girl shit, nonsense, doesn't matter as long as I can vibe to it," I said watching the road as we drove.

"Interesting. Do you like The Weeknd?" she asked.

"Yes, of course! His mixtapes are my shit! Their classics in the making." I said enthusiastically sitting up in my seat. The Weeknd was becoming one of my favorite artists. I annoyed Jeffrey with how much I played him when he was anonymous. His music was dark yet sexy and mysterious, I absolutely loved it.

"I loved him when he first dropped, he's a little mainstream now. The money and fame changed his sound. He's all popish now. I prefer the depression, money, sex, and drugs.", she grinned browsing through her phone while trying to pay attention to the road, "This right here is my shit, it's such a sexy ass song." She said as the beat dropped to the song *"What You need"*. She turned the volume up making the car rumble from the bass of the song.

"I just want to take you there, he don't got to nowhere, does he touch you here, this, this, let me take the friction from your lips."

I reminisced on our short-lived intimate moment. I noticed my ears getting hot. I was embarrassed with lust as I shifted my legs trying to calm myself. It was useless, she was doing this on purpose. She made sure to study me from the corner of her eye.

"Yeah...I like this song too..." I said keeping my eyes focused out the window, trying my best to hide how turned one I was.

The sexual tension was building as we rode the rest of the way in silence listening to a sensual playlist. I tried my best to brush it off, constantly reminding myself to text Jeffrey. This was my attempt to keep in touch with the reality of being very married. He was what I needed at the forefront of my mind, not this woman trying to seduce me.

We finally made it to the venue as I watched a small crowd of people gathered slowly filing into the building. Katt drove into the closest parking garage. As she parked, she paused to look at me unbuckling my seat belt. She stared as I asked "What?".

She shrugged her shoulders then smiled while unbuckling herself as we exited the luxurious vehicle. We took a short elevator ride down to the sidewalk, making our way to the venue in silence. She was magnetic as people began to recognize her the closer we got. Once we were in the building, she introduced me to her friend who set the entire event up. He was a black hipster named Jabo. He was tall maybe six feet, skinny frame, looking stoned as I assumed he smoked on the regular.

"Katt, honey, thank you for letting me do this. You know I love you and all your work. This is amazing. You came through in the clutch, lord knows I needed this.", he said greeting her with a hug and kiss. Katt expressed her gratitude while introducing us.

All her pieces were amazing. As I'd secretly hoped, I spotted the paintings of myself front and center. I watched people admire the series of paintings in as much awe as I was of her artistic expression. At one point, she grasped my hand causing me to pull away, making her chuckle as she side eyed me.

"Here she goes trying to seduce me again?" I thought to myself. She wanted me and played little to no games about her desires. I watched her command the room, conversing with anyone analyzing or interested in her work. It appeared she sold quite a few pieces.

She was in her element as the main event of the night, charismatically telling the stories that inspired her work. The crowd gathered listening intently, nursing their glasses of champagne and wine.

The night went by fast and before I knew it, the show was over. Katt and Jabo said their goodbyes. They hugged each other so tight that appear to be smothering each other, with love of course. He slipped a envelope in her as we waved goodbye beginning our journey to the parking garage.

"Phew, that went so well! Did you have a good time? Those paintings of you sold out! I'm surprised no one recognized you!"

"Yes, I had a great time, it was cool. I wouldn't expect anyone to notice me, I'm low key unless we're in the gym. It was a different experience for sure." I said blushing. This made her laugh as we found the car. She always seemed amused at how nervous she made me.

"Are you up for the club? This is around the time things start popping off!" she asked as we jumped in the car, buckling ourselves in. I noticed it was going on eleven o'clock.

"Aww, no, clubs aren't my thing. They haven't been since my navy days, even then, I did it to fit in." I confessed as she started the car while grabbing her phone for the GPS.

"Look, I understand that but I'm telling you, I have the perfect spot. It's for people our age with our energy level. Not that young rachet shit. It's a sophisticated club." She said trying to convince me.

"Sophisticated? I'm guessing that means it's for old people?"

"You're absolutely right, it's an old folks club. Old folks are chill, plus they play all the slow jams, all the R&B you could ever wish for."

"It's kind of late, my hus-" she interrupted before I could finish my excuse.

"I'm almost sure your husband is going to be fine knowing you are enjoying yourself with a new friend. I mean goddamn, do you'll wipe each other asses or something?" she joked but I took offense.

"Naw, I just think I need to keep reminding you that I am in fact married." I rolled my eyes while crossing my arms to show my disapproval of that careless joke. She noticed I was irritated and began to apologize.

"Listen, my bad. I just think you should have more fun. It's cool you're married, but I don't think you should miss out on hanging out! Kicking it with your girl wouldn't hurt from time to time. I feel like the hubby will survive without you for a night." She said glancing at me.

I thought about. I honestly didn't miss *hanging out* especially at clubs but I enjoyed our time together. The attention she gave was something Jeffery gave me but with a little flavor. A hint of forbidden fruit, if you will. I let out a big sigh, giving in to her philosophy. Jeffrey was indeed fine without me and most importantly trusted me. The only problem I had was trusting myself at this point. Without a second thought I said, "*fuck it.*"

I could afford a longer night out if I stayed in control. I texted Jeffrey letting him know I'd be home late. He replied "Okay, bae just be safe." And that he'd recently made it home. I kept reminding myself why I was so in love with that man. Yet... here I was trying to be friends with a woman I was clearly attracted to, who clearly wanted to play chess in this game of seduction. My only regret was losing that game and realizing too little too late that she was a mad queen in disguise.

"You let the hubby know you coming home late?

"Yes."

"So Jabo, gave me a little something, something before we left. I know you personal trainers are all about the "*purity of the body*" bullshit, but I think everyone has dabbled with a little weed at some point in their life."

"Katt, I can't. I've never smoked weed a day in my life."

"I know you've seen the movie Friday? You can't be black if you never have. Well, it's not Friday but I'm most definitely trying to free your mind because you ain't got shit else to do! I'm sure the hubby won't mind or even notice. Plus, before you know it, it will be out of your system because you work out so much. And I know you don't have to worry about drug testing from your job, so you're good. Al, just for once in your boring life take a chance. I promise, you won't regret it."

She watched as I pondered.

"Are you sure?" I asked hesitantly.

"I'm positive. All we need to do is take a few hits then head to the club." She said expertly rolling a blunt. She prepared it so quick, I had no choice but to go along with this smoke session. For the first time in my life, I took a few puffs of marijuana. I had an immediate feeling of euphoria that no work out could ever provide. It was different. It was exciting. Katt captured me in her spell. It didn't matter if it was a one-time thing, I was becoming trapped in the web of Katt Murphey.

Chapter 8

We drove to downtown Norfolk, listening to a slew of sensual R&B hits on shuffle. I glanced at Katt in her red dress, trying to figure out how she was still so energetic after mingling all night. She was still hype from her show half the night while celebrating with hits of weed. Then I recalled her having trouble sleeping. I assumed these kinds of activities didn't affect her the way they affected normal people like me.

We arrived to the twenty-five and up club, struggling to find a parking garage that wasn't full. The name of the club, I couldn't quite remember. Ladies were free after eleven, so we walked right in, no problems.

The scene was of people my age and older, I'd say maybe mid to late 30's. They seemed mellow, sitting in booths that surrounded the dance floor. It was 90's night, the DJ had SWV's Weak playing while we strolled through, watching the club sway and sing along to the classic. Katt scanned the room, her eyes low and blood shot red, for somewhere to sit. My high was in full effect as she led me to an empty booth that was hidden in the cut. We took a seat continuing to observe the scene. This my kind of crowd. I hadn't been to a club in years, but this was the first time I was enjoying myself. The music was my speed and the people were mature. It could have been the weed, no I'm sure it was the weed. I felt my eyes low, watching Katt scrolling through her phone bobbing her head to the music. I glanced at mine to see if Jeffrey sent any additional messages, then stored for the rest of the night in my small pocket purse.

"I'm about to get a drink, you should have at least one." She suggested standing to slide from the booth while adjusting her dress.

"You're trying to get me fucked up huh?" I felt the words exiting my lips in slow motion.

She laughed, "Not at all, how many times do I have to tell you! You deserve to have a good time!"

"Ok, this is against my better judgement, but I'll take just ONE drink and nothing hard. It messes with my stomach the next day." I said looking up at her as she pulled money from her purse. She shot me a buzzed smiled then walked to the bar. She came back with what looked like two cosmopolitans. I thought to myself, *"What is this? Sex and the city?"*

"These were the only drinks I could think of that wouldn't get you anymore fucked up. Don't judge me, I love Carrie Bradshaw, she's a low-key problematic inspiration of a white woman!" She laughed handing me the sleek drink while sliding back into our booth. There was an awkward silence between us as we watched people swarm the dance floor. They would come and go as the songs changed. I began to vibe out, enjoying my high along with my drink. This was the first time in a while I was relaxed. My life seemed to revolve around my clients and husband, I forgot what it was like to simply chill. That moment didn't last for long because Katt Murphey began with her lovely bullshit.

"Listen, I feel like I make you uncomfortable." She confessed leaning towards me causing our shoulders touched.

"Yea, you do...I've never had a client kiss me, then want to be friends." I countered cuffing my drink with both hands.

"I mean, like I said it was the pills...and maybe your just sexy as hell to me..." she said with a wink.

"*Here we go again*" I thought to myself as I shifted away from her, but that prompted her to move closer.

"I come on strong... and like I said, I respect the fact you're married, but I know you want me like I want you. You can't hide that."

"I'm not hiding anything. You're a client and soon to be ex friend if you don't stop." I warned slurring my words. She didn't take me serious at all.

"Oh, whatever Al. Your high-yellow ass is turning red as we speak, look at you...slurring your words and whatnot...the weed hittin huh? All you have to do is let me touch it..." she said sitting her drink down to gradually move her hand up my thigh. This all seemed too familiar.

"No, you need to calm down. I don't know what you think this is, but I'm not on that... I thought we were trying to be friends or is that something you say to get in girl's pants?" I said pushing her hand away, yet secretly wanting to pull it closer.

"I'm not trying to get in your pants, I'm trying to get in your pussy.", she snickered, "I think your pussy would be magical. The idea is driving me crazy..." she said getting up for another drink.

I was speechless but I'm sure my flushed face spoke volumes. I wanted to leave but my curiosity convinced me to stay. Jeffrey hadn't said anything remotely that sexual to me in years. A normal person would have gotten out of there for fear of what might happen next. At this point I was no longer a normal person.

She danced back with two more Cosmo's, increasing her level of seduction by the second. I tried not to stare at her as she handed me another drink. I couldn't remember asking for it but accepted it now in autopilot. She watched me as I sipped, then our eyes locked. It was an intense moment. As we began to go further, the beat to Toni Braxton's *You're Making Me High* dropped, that's when Katt lost her it.

"Ohhhh girl, this is my damn song! Ha! How ironic!? Come on, get up! I have to dance to this!" She said jumping up from the booth while grabbing my hand to pull me to follow her. I winced.

"Wait, I can't dance..." I said embarrassed, this stopped her in her tracks as she let out a shrill of laughter.

"How are you married, fucking a WHOLE man, but can't dance?! You know it takes rhythm to fuck right? The sex must not be so great!" she laughed while continuing to force me up. I wasn't sure if I should have been offended or not. Everything was delayed because I was now intoxicated. I managed to get up from the booth though.

"Lemme teach you a little something then..." she said guiding me to the dance floor as I followed sheepishly. I only attempted dancing once before during an eighth-grade dance. I was made fun of so bad that I decided to be a wall flower for the rest of my life. My navy friends understood this when we use to club hop and never pressed me on the issue. Yet here I was with this woman insisting that I move to the beat of a song I also loved.

We made our way to the dance floor as she moved to the beat guiding me to get me to follow her steps. It was useless, I was rhythmless with my head being the only part of my body on beat. She chuckled, unphased at how awful I was, she even pulled me closer, resting her hands on the top of my waist. In this moment, I allowed her to lead as she turned around to shimmy her ass on my crotch. I didn't recall Toni Braxton doing that her in her video, but I went along with it scanning the room to see if anyone was watching us.

"I thought you were supposed to be teaching me something?" I reminded her as she grinded on my pelvis. She laughed still dancing to the beat in her tight red dress and heels. She elegantly moved her hands from my waist to top my shoulders, singing along to the song. She looked me in my eyes as she shifted to my ear whispering the lyrics, "*Oh, I get so high, when I'm around you baby, I can touch the sky, you make my temperature rise, you're making me highhh baby, baby, baby, BABY!*".

I admit I was enjoying the attention; I even began to get on beat with her sways. For the first time in my life, I wasn't self-conscious about my dance moves. It made me think as to why Jeffrey never took the time to help me dance. He liked to dance too. I guess he accepted that about me instead of trying to coach me like Katt. I thought this was fun and it could have been fun with Jeffrey if he'd put some effort into it.

I was feeling the effects from the combination weed and cosmos. I was relaxed while in tune with her as we danced. I managed to forget about the wedding ring on my finger. I'd never felt like this a day in my life, it scared me to death. That feeling ceased to exist when she planted a kiss on my lips for the second time.

The song was slowing down as I returned the kiss. All of her hard work was paying off because I softly grasped her face to introduce my tongue in her mouth. It was like kissing Jeffrey but with less hair and softer lips. The song faded out, that's when I came back to my senses, gingerly pulling myself away from her. She smiled, biting her bottom lip then grabbed my hand, "Come on, let's go to the bathroom before we get out of here..." she said leading the way.

It was like I was in a trance, unaware of the time, stuck in this moment absolute lust. There was no longer confusion or resistance on my part. I wanted Katt and this was the night I was going to have her. Jeffrey was absent from my train of thought. I knew we were heading to the bathroom for more than one type of release.

"You should know, I lied about those pills being the reason I kissed you the first time," She said as we made our way through the door, "And I honestly don't give a fuck about your husband, but you know that..." She said pulling me into a bathroom stall, tossing me against the wall, and quickly locking the thin door behind us. I stumbled, trying to keep my balance.

We began passionately kissing and groping each other. She turned me around, so my butt was pressed against her crotch while furiously kissing and sucking on my neck. A quiet moan escaped my mouth which drove her crazy. She whispered in my ear as she kissed it, "Are you going to let me touch it now?"

Before I could give her an answer, she moved her right hand up my dress, pushing my panties to the side, sliding her fingers inside me. Jeffrey had fingered in vain me for years but never standing up and NEVER in a public place. She made it a point to find my clitoris, wasting no time in the art of stimulation. Slow then fast circular motions, all the while dipping her fingers in and out of me. I let out a uncontrollable moan of passion as I climaxed, legs shaking, while she held me with her fingers still in inside me, trying to cover my mouth with her free hand.

She continued kissing my neck as we both panted with excitement. It wasn't until we heard someone stumble in the bathroom with us that we began to frantically gather ourselves. She took her hand from under my dress. The lady who walked in stumbled into the stall next to us. She relieved herself while drunkenly mumbling. We heard a group of her friends come in after to make sure she was okay. We look at each other quietly giggling. Katt snuck in another kiss. We waited until the ladies was done washing their hands before we stepped out of the stall. We checked each other in the bathroom mirror. The perfect bun I made on top of my head was becoming undone. I started to fix it, but Katt stopped me, moving my hands away from head.

"Just let it hang." She said taking it down while staring at me through the mirror. My cheeks were a pink. I couldn't look her in the eyes for too long, the shame started to creep up.

"The hell just happened? Why was it so good?" I thought to myself, while watching Katt.

She washed her hands, straightened her dress, and fluffed her hair. Her makeup was still intact as she observed a little bead of sweat on her nose that she dabbed away with a paper towel. She was indeed pleased with herself; it was written over her beautiful face. I was pleased as well while trying to contain my guilt. We left the bathroom remembering we left our purses unattended. Luckily, they were safe at out booth.

The substances of the night began to wear off as we were leaving the club. I finally glanced at my phone. It was going on one in the morning as I read Jeffrey's message, *"Hey babe, just checking on you. It's late, hope you're safe."* I winced becoming more disappointed in myself.

Katt and I were silent as we drove back to her place. She smiled the entire drive continued to be pleased with herself. There was no resemblance of shame in her body language. When we pulled in her driveway, I exited the car slowly, still pulsating from the orgasm I had almost forty minutes ago. Katt followed from the driver's seat asking me if I was okay to drive.

"You can stay here if you can't drive home..." she suggested.

"No, I think I'll make it...I'm good." I said opening my car door trying to avoid eye contact with her.

"I know I had you out late, but are we still on for our session tomorrow? I know for a fact weed and Cosmo's won't slow ME down." She asked walking backwards to her front door before I sat in my car. It wasn't going to slow me down either. I felt fine considering I should have been more messed up than I was. I guess it was leaving me system fast for some reason. I'd make sure when I got home to guzzled down some water to be sure. I confirmed to her we were still good of our workout session tomorrow.

"Cool, I'll see you then..." She said entering her home as I watched.

The drive home was me reliving the night. She made me come so hard in such a public place. It was revitalizing. This was something I begged Jeffrey for. She provided this for me assuming it was what I longed for. I felt bad, but also excited for the possibility of more moments like that come. We crossed a line that we should have never cross.

I arrived home to find Jeffrey sound asleep in bed. I decided to wash the filth of the night from my body and climbed in bed next to him. He woke to wrap his arm around me and kiss my cheek. He was the sweetest man I've ever known. He was the only man I ever loved. Why was my body somewhere it shouldn't have been? With someone it shouldn't have been with? Why did I enjoy every single moment of it? I kissed Jeffrey's hand and laid there until my mind let me fall sleep.

Chapter 9

I remained in silence the next day with Jeffrey. I couldn't look at him but he didn't notice. I avoided him in the house, quickly answering any little questions he had. He seemed preoccupied anyway. His job was trying to get him to work overtime, but he refused. He ended up doing some work from his home office. I packed my bag for my appointment with Katt. I wanted to cancel on her and tell Jeffrey everything. That noble thought quickly died when I thought about last night's bathroom visit. I popped my head into Jeffrey's office as he was on a conference call with his coworkers. I stepped to him to get his attention, signaling that I was leaving. He made sure to give kiss my hand before I left. I felt dirty lying to him, however the deception only fueled my sick lust.

"What is wrong with me?"

I made it to Katt's house same time as always. She was dressed in some pink and blue workout gear. No surprise wine bottles waiting to be opened or already opened. She greeted me professionally with her beautiful smile. I guessed that today was going to be a professional day and I could live with that. However, that was wishful thinking. Immediately after I sat my bag down, she began with her lovely bullshit.

"You know... I wish I hadn't washed my hands last night," she said leaning against her front door. She caught me off guard, I listened as she continued, "I wanted to smell you for the rest of the night." She said crossing her arms.

"I don't know what to say…" I said stunned.

"I do…I want to taste you Allison, I had an appetizer, now I'm ready for the course. Your husband has been selfish with his plate, it's time for him to share." She said looking me up and down for a response. I simply had no words. All I wanted to do was focus on my job yet here we were again. Here I was again in a situation I knew was inevitable.

She walked toward her bedroom, nodding for me to follow. I looked at my gym bag then at the front door, but ultimately gave into my newly discovered desires. She kissed me as she did the night before with me returning the gesture. She caressed my muscular arms while taking the time to admire them. She sat me on her queen size bed, ripping my shirt off, while caressing my breast and kissing me from my lips down to my navel. I ran my fingers through her naturally soft hair as she pulled down my shorts then my panties. I quivered when she took her first taste.

"I knew it…you taste just like honey." She said before putting her entire face my pussy. Sex was never this intense with Jeffrey. I didn't know if it was because I knew it was wrong or because a woman pleasing me in ways my husband never did. It didn't matter as I sat back making sure to enjoy it all. I had the second-best orgasm of my life. It was from the sweet mouth of a dangerous woman.

Chapter 10

The affair went on for months. It became easier to sleep with Katt then come home to kiss my husband. I used the weekdays for sex with him if desired it, often leaving him warn out by the time the weekend rolled around. I made it a point to make sure he never questioned my desire or love for him. I viewed myself as a terrible person. Another first in my life was watching myself become extremely greedy. I received a sick thrill from it all.

Katt wanted to me travel to Chicago with her and begged me for weeks. Since Jeffrey thought we were only friends, he didn't think twice when I told him I was going with her for a weekend. It wasn't a work trip; it was for pleasure. He was so wrapped up in his work that I could have traveled to another country without him noticing.

"Make sure you behave yourself out there." He said kissing me while on the phone before I left to meet Katt.

When we arrived in Chicago, we made it a point to stay downtown. We booked a room at the Congress Hotel. We visited museums, strolled through millennium park, and visited the Willis Tower aka the Sears Tower for true Chicagoans.

We looked like a new couple strolling down Michigan Avenue embracing each other with public displays of affection. It was like we were tourist in our city even though I visited more often than her for work. She recalled old hang out spots and how the cities air was drench with the smell of the local food, she seemed in heaven. We found ourselves at the lakefront as I noticed her mood begin to shift.

"What's wrong?" I asked with my hand on the small of her back. She snapped out of whatever trance she was in returning my concern with a smile.

"Nothing, just memories..." she said kissing me as we took in the breeze from the lake.

She never mentioned her family and I didn't care to ask. I thought it was strange that she was home and didn't want to visit anyone. I didn't want to visit my family for obvious reasons. They'd have too many questions that I didn't want to answer.

I realized this trip was just for *us*. She wanted to get me away from Virginia making sure to have me all to herself. I was fine with this because we fucked in the most public places which satisfied me intensely.

She fucked me in the back of a uber while the driver was trying incredibly hard not to watch through his rearview mirror. He swerved on an intersection which made us laugh hysterically as we continued to kiss and fool around in his back seat. She fucked me again as we sat close in a fancy restaurant making the waiter blush with embarrassment as she did her job. We left her a big tip. She gave me head in an out-of-site corner in the hotel hallway as guest threatened to discover us. It was exhilarating and simply couldn't help myself while undeniably enjoying myself. I must have been temporarily insane to be having a full-blown affair with this woman out int the open with clients throughout the area. It didn't matter for a brief time I wasn't afraid of being caught. The trip was everything to me. I felt free and sexually satisfied on every level. It wasn't until we returned from Chicago, Katt began to change.

One Sunday after we had sex, she became a bit strange. She wanted me to move some of my things in with her. I thought she was joking but she maintained a straight face the entire time while suggesting. I reminded her that we weren't in a relationship and that I still in fact had an entire husband. This sent her into an unexpected rage.

"What do I look like to you? Some kind of well-kept secret Al? I can call your husband right now! I can tell him how I just licked the juices dry from your pussy and you loved every second of it! I'll tell him how I had your ass tied to my bed and fucked you with a dick 5 times bigger than he's! I bet he'd love to hear that!" She yelled still nude posted in the middle of her bed. I rushed to clothed myself trying to make my exit. I never witnessed her this upset before. It was upsetting and frightening. It felt like this was all coming from nowhere too. I was under the impression that we were just having fun.

"You're not going to tell my husband anything! You knew what you were doing from the start. You knew what it was and what we were doing. I remember trying to keep it professional from the start or did you forget that when my pussy hit your mouth?" I defended myself.

"Don't act like I just seduced your buff ass, you wanted it and me, but you try to hide behind your pathetic ass husband!" She insulted me and my love for Jeffrey. Now she was being disrespectful. I was done listening to her nonsense and finally made my way towards the front door making sure not to forget my gym bag. She rushed behind me still naked but draped in her bed sheets. She shoved me causing me stumble but I caught my balance before turning to her. *This bitch is letting her crazy slip out.*

"The hell is your problem Katt? Like why today? What the hell is wrong with? Don't push me again." I questioned while I balled my fist taking a step towards her. She stepped back as tears formed in her eyes. The tears caused me to soften my stance.

"You don't understand Allison...I can't do this with you anymore. I'm not about to be your secret or quick thrill. I want you...I need you and not just on weekends...Ever since I met you, you're all I can think about, do you understand me? My art is a thousand times better since I met you! You're the reason I'm thriving...I...I love you...do you understand? I love you..." She tearfully confessed. My jaw dropped. The entire time we were messing around, love never entered my train of thought. It was the last thing I would have ever thought would develop between us. I liked her, I enjoyed her company, but I can't say I was falling in love with her. Yet, here she was telling me she was in love with me and I couldn't for the life of me understand why or how?

"You can't be serious right now?" I ask astonished. That was not the answer she was hoping for. Her tears returned to rage as she began smacking her head yelling in frustration. For the first time I saw that deranged look in her eyes. Oddly, I still found her attractive wild-eyed and all.

"YOU KNOW WHAT!? GET THE HELL OUT OF MY HOUSE!" she screamed looking for something to throw at me. I made it out the door managing to safely dodge the vase she hurled my way. I dashed to my car with my gym bag securely in hand. I drove off as quickly as I could while she chased behind yelling and cursing.

"What the hell? What the hell...?" I thought out loud as I sped home.

Chapter 11

I was disturbed for the next few weeks. While I was at worked, I stared at my phone as Katt relentlessly sent me text after text, all of which I ignored. I was a pro at hiding everything from Jeffrey by now, but Nya was a different story. After she interrogated me while we were sitting at our desk, I broke down, confessing everything to her.

"Wow, you really crossed that line and slept with that woman?" she said amazed.

"You were the one that said she could be a little project...I kept that in mind and gave in. It was cool until she flipped out on me. Look, she won't stop texting me." I said showing her all the messages Katt sent within minutes of each other.

"Yea, but I also told you to keep it professional and make a new friend, not keep it professional and fuck a new friend, love!? Now we find out this woman is crazy!? Didn't I tell you I should have met her first? I have third eye for crazy bitches." she said as I remembered her words, but everything with Katt happened so fast. I simply put off introducing her to Nya.

"Yea, you did..." I shamefully agreed.

"It's always the artists that turn out to be bat shit crazy, haven't you seen any movie ever?" she said shaking her head, "Listen, if you need to me handle her, you know I will. Remember I got the law on my side, Todd will gladly falsify police reports on my behalf." She boldly suggested. I looked at her like she was crazy, but I couldn't fault her for having my back.

"I don't think that will solve the problem, fool. I just don't want Jeffrey to find out." I said at that moment regretting ever starting the affair.

"Not responding isn't going to help! You need to tell her to stop and break it off clean! I mean what the hell Al... She chased you BUTT ASS NAKED because you won't leave your husband! It's time for this to be over!" She passionately explained.

"You're right..." I said as I started to type a cease-and-desist message to Katt but was interrupted by her calling my name, catching both Nya's and I attention.

"Oh, shit... What is she doing here?" I stood up in shock. There Katt was standing with her with black shades, signature afro, and wearing a black t-shirt with #GODDESS printed across her chest. She filled out a pair of jeans with all white Nike's to completing her look. She looked so casual while maintaining her breathe taking stature despite her current state of crazy.

"Allison, Allison, Allison, now all of a sudden you can't read text messages?" She said with a grin on her face. It made me uneasy as she strutted towards us waving her phone. Nya stood up, side-eying me, letting me know she was ready to pounce in case Katt were to get out of hand.

"I was about to text you back... We need to talk but not here at my job..." I said stepping from around my desk to guide her outside. Nya watched studying Katt as she studied her back.

"That must be Nya huh? Hmmm, I thought she'd be prettier." She snarled as I grasp her arm to force her out the front door.

"Look, it's one thing to throw shit at me while I'm at your place but it's another thing to show up at my job trying to make a scene Katt!" I said frustrated with her bizarre behavior. She lowered her voice to a timid volume while removing her shades.

"Why weren't you answering my messages?" she quietly asked.

"You didn't give me a chance, you sent like fifty at once and constantly! How am I supposed to respond to that?!" I said pointing to my phone scrolling through the messages for her to see.

"I don't know, maybe call me..." she said prompting me to lose my shit.

"Listen, I'm not going to be calling, or texting, or having you as a client, or a friend anymore! This mess between us is OVER! You're doing entirely too much! I can't have SHIT like this in my life!" I asserted while taking a step back anticipating a violent response.

"NOW you can't have me in your life Al? Even after that weekend we spent in Chicago!? I know for a fact you loved every MINUTE! NOW you don't want this because I love you and need you... WELL FUCK YOU AL! FUCK YOU AND YOUR HUSBAND!" she shouted as she pushed my chest causing me to stumble backwards. That's when Nya bolted from the gym entrance, almost running through Katt with the force of an NFL fullback.

"Yo back the hell up hoe!" she pushed snapping Katt back to reality.

"She must be the real reason why, huh Allison? Tell me Nya, can you suck and fuck the soul out of her pussy like I do, or do you just lay there letting her practice everything I taught her on your boney ass!"

That infuriated Nya causing her to lose complete control. She opened-palmed smacked Katt so hard that her glasses went flying into the parking lot. I grabbed Nya trying desperately to restrain her before she fixed her fist to throw a punch. Katt recollected herself as she stood holding her face, laughing with a devilish grin. She picked recovered her glasses and slid them back on her red face.

"Must have stuck a nerve." She continued to chuckle while grabbing her face.

"Get the hell out of here before I call the cops." I warned still trying to control Nya who was ready for more action.

"Cops don't scare me Al. You're going to regret this..." She threatened walking away. I let Nya go once Katt hopped into her BMW.

"Allison, what the hell?!" she said catching her breathe as we both looked around making sure our supervisor wasn't alerted of the scene. Surprisingly, there wasn't a small crowd to witness the madness that'd just occurred. However, I remembered there was always a security camera recording everything. Someone above my pay grade and possibly the police would see the footage.

I was rattled she showed up to my job. My only thought was *"What if she came to my house?"*. From that point on I was paranoid and frightened, not only of her, but at the thought of Jeffrey finding out what I'd been doing with her this entire time.

Chapter 12

Katt became unhinged after her visit to my job. She started following Jeffrey and I to the grocery store, making sure I saw her making vulgar gestures with her mouth to symbolize giving oral sex while Jeffrey wasn't looking. She made it a point to show she knew where we lived by parking outside our home. She routinely appeared at my job, sitting outside on her car waiting for a moment to catch me alone, but Nya wasn't having it.

Nya pleaded with me to tell Jeffrey everything. She wanted to get her cop boyfriend involved, suggesting I file a restraining order. I was reluctant until Katt became bold enough to bust out my car windows at work. I had no idea how I was going to explain that to Jeffrey. Once he saw my car, he was worried and angry, but I continued to lie telling him someone mistook my car for one of their ex-lovers. He hesitant in believing me, but it would be a matter of time before he began asking more questions.

The way he began to look at me was changing as well. It was either confess or let things continue to escalate. Rather than confessing my indiscretion's I continued to endure Katt Murphey's harassment.

One day, I made it a point to allude her while driving home. I caught her BMW tailing me in my rearview mirror. We sped through intersections swerving through traffic until I had enough and managed to pull into a gas station to confront her. She violently pulled up behind me as I parked my car, running directly to my now repaired window, banging on the glass and yelling, "FUCK YOU AL, FUCK YOU! YOU KNOW I LOVE YOU! THIS CAN ALL STOP IF YOU JUST COME WITH ME! BE WITH ME!"

I watched in horror trying to convince her to back away so I could get out from the car. I knew I was taking a risk exiting the safety of my car, that's why I calmly grabbed my taser, and slid it in my pocket before I stepped out. She stood there in hysterics but calmed down crossing her arms as I stared at her.

"Why are you acting like this Katt? You need to stop! You could have killed us driving like that! You could have hurt innocent people! How can you say you love me, but harass me like this? You need to stop!" I said firmly trying to hide my fear.

"No! you need to stop acting like I don't mean anything to you!" she shouted.

"But...Katt...you don't...I tried to be friends with you, but you don't get it...I'm sorry I crossed that line with you...that was my mistake, it was fun, it was different for me...but I don't feel the same way for you..." I confessed observing the second time I saw that deranged look in her eyes as she began charging toward me. I quickly drew my taser shocking her in the neck. She convulsed as she fell to the ground while bystanders began to form a crowd. I looked around praying no one was recording before jumping back into my car and fleeing the scene. That was the last straw. I decided to get in contact with Nya's cop boyfriend to finally file a restraining order against her.

It was wishful thinking to hope no one was recording the chaos, but one of Jeffrey's coworkers who was on a gas run and posted the commotion on his Facebook live. He showed it to him when he got back to the office. When I got home after filing the restraining order, Jeffrey confronted me telling me he had to convince his coworker to take the video down for the sake of my businesses. I was left with the task of explaining who the woman was in the video because he'd never met Katt. I had to confess that I had an affair with her and she became obsessed with the idea of us separating. I told him I was trying to protect him and our marriage which angered him.

"PROTECT ME? PROTECT ME? HOW IS FUCKING SOME RANDOM WOMAN BEHIND MY BACK PROTECTING ME!" he yelled as I sat in shame on our couch.

"Jeffrey, listen..." I began to explain.

"No! I don't have to listen to shit! FUCK! It all makes since now! You thought I was so fucking stupid! You thought I wasn't paying attention! I knew something was off with you from the very beginning when you took her on as a client! What...when...that time... Were you fucking me like that because you were guilty!? WHAT THE FUCK!? HOW COULD YOU DO THIS TO ME?! TO US?" he yelled pacing the room while coming to the realization that I was a terrible human being.

"Jeffrey, please...just let me explain...I am so sorry. I love you...I love you" I pleaded.

"Love me? So, did you love while you were out fucking your client? The trip to Chicago? You fucked her the entire time there too didn't you!? DIDN'T YOU?" he yelled infuriated. I'd never seen my husband this was before but it was understandable. I felt like shit knowing I hurt him to his core.

The entire time I assumed he wasn't paying attention to me, when he in fact, he was far more in tuned with me than I'd ever gave him credit for.

"I just needed something different... I was still with you...I'm still with you..." I whimpered trying to justify my selfish act. He wasn't hearing it.

"I have to get the hell out of here! Don't follow me and DON'T CALL ME!" he shouted grabbing his keys and storming out the door. I was left there with my tears. I was in disbelief of what just occured. I should have never crossed the line with Katt. I was now paying for it with the loss of the love of my life. I tried so desperately to protect him by deceiving him every chance I had. I laid in bed that night crying myself to sleep, hurt, scared, and paranoid.

Chapter 13

Two weeks went by after Jeffrey stormed out. He made it a point to get his things little by little while I wasn't home. It was hard to concentrate on work and I despised traveling out of town for clients. I was distraught from it all. My world was literally falling apart. My supervisor suggested I take a few days off to get myself together. I hadn't heard or seen anything from Katt since I tased her and filed the restraining order.

Nya checked on me every chance she had. She told me Todd did a background check on Katt and found nothing. She was clean of any criminal behavior. Nya took it upon herself to dig deeper. She discovered her ex-boyfriend was now in a wheelchair and lived in a secluded home in Suffolk, Va. Her investigation skills also revealed he was stabbed in the back and was paralyzed from the waist down. She contacted him trying to ask about Katt, but he cursed her out saying he would press charges for harassment if she ever called again.

It was clear now, Katt Murphey was extremely dangerous. Without Jeffrey, and Nya working, I was afraid to go anywhere by myself. I was also afraid to stay home alone. I feared having a restraining order wasn't going to stop Katt from getting to me and showing me how much she *really* loved me. I asked myself how I could make such a mess of my life. I went from having an amazing husband, but being bored in the bedroom, to having a salacious affair, to having no husband and a crazy bitch coming after me... It didn't make sense. I couldn't have been more disappointed with myself.

Chapter 14

Now that you're all caught up, here is how I ended up in Katt's home bound to a chair.

I was home taking a personal day my supervisor recommended, up late watching trash tv trying to distract mind from Jeffrey being gone by attempting to laugh. I missed him. I longed for him to come back home, but I respected his wishes to not communicate. He required time which I completely understood.

I was texting Nya until she stopped responding which told me she'd fallen asleep. Out of nowhere, I received a text from Jeffrey. It read *"We need to talk."* I eagerly text back telling him I was willing to do anything to hear his voice. He told me to meet him at a location close to Chesapeake mall which is where we often shopped for clothes. It was about one in the morning, but no red flags went off for me as to why he wanted to meet so late. Jeffrey was more of a day person and wouldn't do anything past six o'clock. However, I was blinded by my excitement, my husband desired to talk to me. I dropped everything I was doing, hopped in my car, and sped out of our driveway.

I pulled into the parking lot of an abandoned Toys R Us and saw his car parked with the lights off. That was the second red flag I ignored. I parked my car in front of he's, pausing for a moment to see if he was in his car. I saw the silhouette of him sitting in the driver seat. Without thinking, I turned off my car, hurrying over to open his passenger door thinking I would see him scrolling through his phone. Instead, to my surprise, I saw him passed out with a gash on his forehead freshly bleeding. He had duct tape covering his mouth with his hands taped together in front of him. I gasped, taking a step back from the car then BAM!

That was all I remembered before I dipped in and out of consciousness while being dragged by my arms. Then everything went completely black.

I'm not sure how she managed to do it all without anyone witnessing but she did. I was scared senseless as I began to wake. I came to only to find her holding a combat knife to my neck.

"You know...we could have been so fuckin perfect together...but you had to FUCK it up!"

My head was still throbbing from whatever she knocked me out with. I felt stinging on my heels from her dragging me to this point. I anxiously looked around, trying to decode my surroundings, but was interrupted by her snatching my face. She forced me to look her in the eyes.

"You have been trying to sabotage everything between us Al, I just want to understand...Please help me understand because I LOVE YOU!" she said with that deranged look in her eyes I had seen twice before. This was the final time and I was terrified.

"Katt...before you do anything crazy, please calm down... tell me...where are we?" I begged trying to sooth her madness while inconspicuously trying to loosen the duct tape she had around my hands.

"Oh, you don't recognize where we are? This is where we first made love...the first time I had the pleasure of tasting you..." she said stepping away to reveal the home I'd seen several times before. It was usually immaculate, not a piece of anything out of place but was now a disaster, representing the current state of mind my once well put together lover.

"Listen, I know you're upset, but can we talk about this? Where is he?" I begged still trying to loosen the tape.

"That's the thing Al, I'm done talking...and don't worry about him... if I can't have you...no one can." She said as her voice trembled while waiving the knife she once held to my neck. Once again, she knocked me out.

Chapter 15

I awoke again to peaks of light shining in from the curtains indicating the sun was rising. I heard Jeffrey screaming in pain. I assumed they were either in her bedroom or the spare bedroom. Lord knows what she was doing to him. I frantically tried loosening the tape from around my wrist to no avail. I begin sobbing, then with everything in me I yelled, "KATT STOP! PLEASE STOP!"

That's when Jeffrey's screams stopped. I heard her walk from the room shutting the door behind her. She was bare foot as she walked in the living room with my husband's blood covering the coverall's she painted in. I watched in my horror as she approached while she calmly wiped the combat knife off on herself.

"I thought I told you I was done talking Al." she said caressing my hair with her semi-bloody hand.

"Please Katt, he has nothing to do with this, please let him go...let him go then we can be together." I begged gazing up at her. She starred at me with a blank face, then had a rush of relief wash over her.

"I can't believe I had to do this again...I just can't believe it..." She started to confess, "I should have mentioned to you, when I fall in love, I fall hard. I can't help myself. It's been like this since I was little."

"You never mentioned that to me...you said you were depressed as a kid."

"I was and for a long time because everyone I loved didn't love me back, I had to be put away Al."

"What do you mean?" I asked still trying to hide my fear, "Listen, Katt, you can tell me anything" I assured her. She glanced at me, then placed her bloody knife on the kitchen counter. She pulled up a chair, sat down while letting out a long sigh, and stroked her hair back.

"When I was seventeen, I figured out I like girls... I struggled with depression, I struggled with my art, now I had to struggle with my sexuality. It was too much. One day I went to the lakefront with my paint brushes and decided jumping over wouldn't have been so bad. I threw my paint brushes in first and watched as they hit the water, slowly floated away. Then it was my turn. As I began to climb over, I heard the sweetest voice yell "Hold on babe! You don't want to do that!" and there she was like a guardian angel..." She said smiling as she reminisced.

"Who was it?" I asked trying to keep her in this calm state while slowly fidgeting with my restraints the entire time.

"It was Angela. She was the most beautiful creature I'd ever seen."

In my head I thought *"had?"*.

"She was your first girlfriend?"

"Yea, my first real everything... she saved my life, she helped me get my life back together. She helped me get better during my stay at the mental hospital. It took a year for me to get better. I had to get better Al, I couldn't be out there suicidal and shit. My parents made sure those records went away if you know what I mean? They weren't always present for everything in my life, but they made sure I didn't taint their good name." She laughed. I smirked uncomfortably, then asked the question that needed to be answered.

"What happened to Angela?"

She went from smirking to emotionless as she crossed her arms, making sure to sit up straight in the chair.

"Well, after 3 years, Angela decided rather than telling me she didn't want to be with me anymore, she would just cheat. It left me heartbroken but I STILL LOVED HER AL! Now I'll admit showing up to her job, chasing her up and down those Chicago streets didn't make things any better, but she had to understand how much I loved her, like I love you Al. It's not easy for me to fall back and stop caring about someone. It's not easy at all, do you understand? I couldn't let her be with anyone else. It just wasn't going to happen." She explained.

"So, what happened to her Katt?" I asked again. She looked at me tilting her head letting out another long sigh.

"She said she was leaving Chicago and wanted to end all communication, sound familiar huh? Anyway, I begged her to meet at the Lake where she saved my life... she took an unfortunate dunk in the water...they found her body a couple of days later, Al. It was the saddest shit ever." She confessed covering her face to hide what I presumed was guilt. I sat in shock prompting me to ask another hard question.

"What about your ex-boyfriend, you know, the one who also cheated on you?" I asked remembering what Nya discovered. That's when a devilish grin took over her face.

"Let's just say, he'll never be able to use his dick again." She laughed, "that idiot had it coming too...I never told you I caught him red handed screwing some sailor chick in my bed next to my damn art Al! Not only did he disrespect me, but he disrespected my ART!" she stood up shouting, "Let me show you what was hanging in my bedroom." She said before jogging to the garage.

I watched until she was out of site, violently shaking my hands, using my nails to try get a break in the tape. The kitchen counter was too far for me to scoot and grab the knife without her noticing. I prayed in my head, continuously working at getting a tiny slit in the tape. She returned with a portrait of a face of a light skinned woman resembling me. It was on a huge canvas she struggled to drag, possibly one of the ones covered in the garage. The resemblance between us was strikingly disturbing, the only differences were our nose.

"He disrespected Angela, Al. I couldn't have that. I know he's learned his lesson now." She said as she stroked the face on the canvas. She then sat it on the couch, staring at it before turning her attention back to me.

"When I saw you on Instagram, you reminded me so much of her, I couldn't resist. I had to get to know you, I had to have you in my life. It's amazing to me how similar you both are. Angela was into art like me, but you with your fitness! God! You guys share that same passion for the things you love. That shit drives me crazy! It gets me so wet!" she said caressing my neck with one hand while feeling herself with the other. I finally got the slit in the tape and began to tear it apart little by little with her none the wiser. I continued to distract her, trying to give myself enough time and trying keep her from torturing Jeffrey.

"You must have passion for the things you love or what's the point, right?" I said making eye contact with her.

"Yes, of course, I don't understand why no one can feel that same passion for me." She said standing over me, "I hate that your husband has to be involved Al, but he is in the way! He's in our way because I know you love me! You have too!"

"Yes, Katt I do love you! You just took things too far! How was I supposed to leave Jeffrey when you didn't give me any time?" I tried convincing her, "You should have been patient, I heard you, I understood you wanted us to be together."

"Then why did you act like that? Why the fuck did you tase me!" she said as angry overtook her, "That shit hurt AL, I pissed myself in that damn parking lot!"

"I didn't know what was coming, I was scared but it didn't stop me from caring about you. I had to push you away to give myself time, time to get rid of Jeffrey and time to get my shit and move on... I just needed time..." I said finally getting a hand free while she began to pace.

"Yes, yes, HA! It all makes sense! That's why he was moving into that apartment when I snatched him up! You broke the news to him! AWK! Why didn't I think about that!?" she said stopping to smack herself on the head as her delusional began to make sense.

"How did you find him?" I asked still trying to keep her distracted.

"Remember when I told you I was an artist among other things...well, yea the other things are special skills I acquired through YouTube." She shrugged.

"YouTube?" I countered puzzled.

"Yea, duh, you can learn anything from Youtube." She said amazed at my confusion.

"Oh shit, I guess you're right...but you didn't have to kidnapped him Katt."

"Yes, I did but knowing this, there's no point in living in the past Allison! He has to go for good for us to be together!" she declared turning to pick up the combat knife she'd terrorized us with. That's when I yelled "NO!" springing from the chair to grab her.

I pushed her forcing her to drop the knife. It flew on the kitchen floor as I pinned her on the counter from behind. I struggled to turn her around as she flailed trying to hit me. I pushed her again trying to knock some wind out of her, but she was resilient as she turned around to smack my face causing me to stumble. I recuperated, grabbing her as she searched for the knife. I punched her in the neck causing her to scream out in pain. I searched for the knife while she grasped her neck in agony. She pulled my hair, flinging me on my back, then kicked me in the stomach while I was down.

"All that muscle and can't do shit with it!" she teased pushing her hair back before kicking me again, knocking the wind out of me. I struggled at catching my breath but noticed her foot close to my hand and without thinking, I tripped her. She fell violently on her face, bursting her bottom lip. She groaned before countering with a kick to me face, bursting my nose upon impact. I winced, grabbing at my nose, still trying to catch my breath. That's when we both spotted the knife. We struggled to crawl towards it, kicking and punching each other the entire way. That's when I took it upon myself to use my body weight to climb on top of her putting her in a chokehold.

She tried to stop me from wrapping my right forearm around her neck, but I overpowered her.

"I guess these muscles can do something bitch!" I said squeezing as tight as I could until I felt her go limp. That wasn't enough for me, so I held on until her breathing was shallow.

"Crazy bitch." I flung her limp body, finally able to catch my breath. I grabbed the knife and ran for Jeffrey. I burst through the door of her master bedroom but he wasn't there. I ran to the other bedroom, discovering my husband tied to a chair shirtless. He had big and tiny cuts across his muscular chest. I winced as he sat motionless. I noticed the cuts weren't deep as he slowly bled. I shook his face causing him to wake in a panic.

"HUH! Please stop! What do you want from me!?" he shouted. I covered his mouth trying to calm him, showing him that it was me not Katt. Once he realized it, he calmed down relieved to see his wife. I began to cut the tape from around his hands as fast as I could.

"What the hell is going on, Allison? Why am I bleeding? Why am I here?" he asked exhausted and examining his chest wounds. There was no time to answer him as I pulled away the last of the tape from around his wrist. I looked for his shirt with no luck, so I pulled him by his shoulders, lifting him from the chair. He slowly regained his strength as we stumbled out of the room making our way to the living room. I looked around for Katt with half his body draped over my shoulder, but she'd vanished.

"Shit! We need to get the hell out of here! She woke back up!" I said hurrying my weak husband to the front door. We both moved as quickly as we could but were stopped by the sound of a gun cocking back.

"Not so fast, my love." Katt stood with a 9mm shaking as blood ran down her mouth.

Jeffrey and I froze. This might be the end of both of us and it was all my fault.

Chapter 16

"You didn't think that weak ass chokehold was going to keep me out long enough for you to leave, did you sweetheart?" she said wiping blood from her chin making sure to keep the gun pointed at both of us.

"Please Katt, please let him go! You want me right!? Just take me!" I pleaded still bearing the weight of Jeffrey over my shoulder. He stood there silent watching Katt's every move.

"I can't let either of you go. You know my secret's...I don't think that will sit well with people in the art world." She laughed as she moved closer with the threat of setting the gun off.

"You're the same person I met for our first session.... what happened to her? She was so nice. She was sweet, she wouldn't have wanted to hurt me. I thought she was a great client." I said backing both Jeffrey and I away from her advance.

"I know and you did get my body right, I thank you for that. I'm sorry it has to end this way...Why couldn't you just be with me Al?" She continued to laugh with every step forward still aiming the gun at us.

"Katt, I told you we can be together...you have to let Jeffrey go, please. Please don't hurt him. I love you." I reasoned with her, this time she wasn't fooled. I took Jeffrey's arm from around my shoulder and pushed him behind me. If anyone was going to die, it was going to me.

"Look at you, you can't possibly love me. you're still trying to protect this piece of shit." She snarled, "I can't have this Allison, I can't have it all. You both can go! You both have to die! HA! You two would make the perfect painting! I'll paint you in those workout clothes you wore the first time we met...yea and I'll paint good old Jeffrey in the background, both of you drenched in blood, yeah, I'll call it "Training Session; Deadly Obsession", it will be my masterpiece! My greatest work to date!" she explained in a villainous monologue as we listened.

I stood in front of Jeffrey, holding his waist from behind listening to him breath. I wanted to remember every breath he took before I died because I was sure Katt was going to pull the trigger. It was destined to end like this. Our lives were going to be taken by my jilted psychotic lover.

I should have never given in to my temptation. I should have ignored the advances of a mysterious woman. I should have taken control of my sex life in my so-called happy marriage. I was filled with so much regret and fear that I closed my eyes, almost sure she was about to pull the trigger. She let off two rounds, one missed us both the other grazed Jeffrey's right shoulder as he screamed in pain.

That's when the front door flew open with police yelling, "FREEZE! DROP YOUR WEAPON!" Before I knew it more shots were fired as Jeffrey and I dropped to the floor taking cover. When the firing stopped, I peeked up to see Nya's boyfriend standing over us offering his hand like Arnold Schwarzenegger in the Terminator Two. I took it because I indeed wanted to live. We helped Jeffrey up while his back up rushed in to provide further assistance. I looked over to where

Katt was once standing pointing the 9mm. Now she laid with several gunshot wounds as a coped kicked the gun from her hand and checked her pulse.

"She's still breathing! Call an ambulance!" he reported.

"Allison!" Nya shouted running as we limped out the door. I was relieved to see her and even more relieved to still be alive. I took a deep breathe. It was finally over...

Chapter 17

"How did you find us?" I asked Nya while sitting down on the edge of the open ambulance door as a paramedic tended to my nose. Jeffrey was inside on a stretcher getting his shoulder and chest examined. He was still in shock from everything.

"Girl, I fell asleep last night with something not sitting well with me. You know it was my woman's intuition! I text you three times this morning and you didn't respond. That's not like you Allison! I begged Todd to do the most illegal shit ever and track your phone. The stupid bitch took your phone with her. I didn't recognize the address he pulled up which confirmed my suspicions. I told Todd to call for back up and we rushed our asses over here! I had to save my girl!" she said pushing the paramedic out the way to hug me. Thank God for friends like Nya. If it weren't for her, we would've died.

We watched as they rolled Katt out to another ambulance waiting at the scene. They were still working on her as she breathed through an oxygen mask.

"Is she going to make it?" I asked a cop.

"I shouldn't say this, but unfortunately, yes. She had two bullets pass through her arms and legs. They were able to get the bleeding under control. I won't know more until she gets to the hospital, but I promise we'll be waiting if she wakes up." He assured.

"Good. She needs to be put the hell away." Nya chimed in.

Jeffrey had to ride to the hospital for further treatment and was released the next day. I nursed him the rest of the way back to health, making sure to apologize every chance I got. It wasn't easy and with the help of therapy, he eventually forgave me.

We endured weekly visits to a marriage counselor and couples sex therapist. At one point, we decided to separate, however, it didn't last long because no matter what, we realized we were made for each other. We continued to make every effort to repair our marriage which rewarded us with our first child.

We continued thriving in our careers with Jeffrey receiving a huge promotion while I was expanding by opening two gyms that ran themselves.

Nya was our child's god mother and my new business partner. Life was amazing. I can honestly say I'd never been happier.

After being treater for her wounds, Katt Murphey was arrested for stalking and attempted murder. She was deemed unfit to stand trail due to extreme psychotic delusions.

The judge sentenced her to a mental health facility in Arlington, Va. It was the second time in her life she'd wound up committed and this time for good. That was the last I'd heard of her.

I felt sad for her. I mourned our affair for a short period while recalling she literally tried to kill me and my husband.

I'd sometimes imagine her sitting in a psych-ward painting portraits of me realizing she would never be well. She was talented painter though.

I wondered if they allowed recreational periods for patients. Maybe I could get a partnership with the gym to give those people some light in their state of darkness. Then again, dealing with an insane person almost cost me my life. I concluded my thoughts of her, vowing to never mix business with pleasure ever again.

Chapter 18

Two years later at an unnamed mental health facility in Arlington, Va......

"Ms. Murphey, it's time for your meds, also you have visitors, your parents I believe." The nurse announced.

"These again...and them again...Nurse Janet, do you know these pills make my pussy dryer than the Sahara Desert? I'm tired of taking this shit."

"I know and I'm sorry Ms. Murphey but you must. You've been doing so well this last year. Don't you want to get out of here and back to your art?"

"Hmph...yea, I guess that's why my parents are here, huh?"

"I'd like to assume. Now take your meds and come down to the visitor's room."

"Alright." I said pretending to swallow the pills with the little ass cup of water they always give me.

I always wondered if Nurse Janet knew I didn't take those pills all the time. When did I did take them, I felt absolutely nothing. They really did make my pussy dry. I could start a damn fire every time I tried to play with myself in this God forsaken place. I wanted OUT!

"Hi Ma, Hi Dad." I said as I pulled up a chair to my studious parents. They were so smug.

"Hello Katherine, how are you doing today?" my dad greeted.

"I'm shitty dad. I'm horny and I want to paint. How an times do I have to tell you to call me Katt!?" I snapped.

My mother cleared her throat shooting me a stern look. That same look always followed with a soft tap of the face when I was a child, but as I got older, I learned to straighten up and fly right.

"Sorry Ma, I'm just tired of being here. I need to get out, it's killing my creativity!" I pleaded.

"Well Katherine, whom do you have to blame but yourself. I thought you worked through these issues. How many times do we have to put in favors to save you? You're an adult for goodness sake. It's time for you to act like one." My mother chastised as she's done my entire life. I hated her.

"Honey we're working on things again. You must remain patient and continue to get better." my father assured.

"Yes, we are working on it. Katherine, this is the last time I want to see you somewhere like this. Do you know how embarrassing it is for your father and I to explain that although our daughter has never wanted for anything and is a gifted artist, she can't seem to keep her crazy in check. This the last time Katherine, I mean it." She said folding her arms in disgust. I took her serious this time.

"Yes mother." I said lowering my head in submission like a well-trained dog.

"It won't be too much longer Kather...Katt. We'll get you some painting materials and make sure the warden understands you need to express yourself. I love you honey. We'll keep updating you, okay." My dad said standing to offer a warm hug as he always had my entire life. My mother remained seated observing our embrace before grabbing her purse and making her way towards the entrance. She peered back silently beckoning my father to join her. He did as he always done before leaving me by applying a kiss to my forehead.

As promised hours later, I received some painting supplies with a modest size canvas to work on. Of course, I was under supervision the entire time as I mixed colors and glanced around as I pondered inspiration for the canvas.

I didn't mean for thing to get so out of control with Al. I didn't mean for things to get out of control with any of my lovers. Ever since I was a child, I've just had so much love in my heart. I wanted to share it, that's all but people can't handle it. That can't handle how I love. That's ot my fault, it's theirs. Obsessive personality and Bi-polar disorder is the diagnoses, but I believe every creative genius has a little "crazy" they have to manage to be great and loved.

I feel like I must tell my story for you to understand. I guess I'll begin with the canvas, one color, one stroke of a brush at a time......

TO BE CONTINUED